COLLINS
Workplace English

辦公室英語
互動篇

James Schofield

商務印書館

Collins 辦公室英語（互動篇）
Collins Workplace English (Business Interaction)

作　　者： James Schofield

責任編輯： 黃家麗

封面設計： 楊愛文

出　　版： 商務印書館（香港）有限公司

香港筲箕灣耀興道 3 號東匯廣場 8 樓

http://www.commercialpress.com.hk

發　　行： 香港聯合書刊物流有限公司

香港新界大埔汀麗路 36 號中華商務印刷大廈 3 字樓

印　　刷： 中華商務彩色印刷有限公司

香港新界大埔汀麗路 36 號中華商務印刷大廈 14 字樓

版　　次： 2015 年 2 月第 1 版第 1 次印刷

©2015 商務印書館（香港）有限公司

ISBN 978 962 07 0378 2

Printed in Hong Kong

版權所有　不得翻印

How to use 如何使用

建議用四十五分鐘至一個小時學習一個單元。全書合共二十四個單元,每週抽出兩個小時學習,可於三個月內完成。

Step 1
先閱讀 Conversation 的英語對話。對話旁邊若標示了 ▶ DVD ,請看相關視像。若標示了 🔊 ,請聆聽相關錄音。

Step 2
使用 Understanding 提供的內容,檢查自己是否已理解英語對話。

Step 3
嘗試回答 Practice 的練習題,並核對答案。

Step 4
按 Speaking 標示 You 的內容講英語,講完之後聆聽播音員的錄音,對比自己講的英語是否準確。

Step 5
參考 Resource bank 的實用資料,如:Translation of conversations、Key phrases for speaking、Key phrases for writing、On the phone — useful phrases、Grammar reference 等。

Step 6
嘗試回答 Grammar reference and practice 的練習題。

Contents 目錄

Face-to-face meetings & video conferencing
當面開會及視像會議

Resource Bank 參考資料

The story 故事

在《Collins 辦公室英語（互動篇）》裏，我們跟着倫敦洛維電子公司項目經理湯姆•菲特的步伐。湯姆現時負責洛維工程公司和澳洲電力公司（APU）的合併項目。APU公司的總部在悉尼，而洛維工程公司正被APU公司收購。除了與洛維工程公司負責合併項目的高級經理（黛安•甘迺迪）交流外，湯姆還要和APU公司的約翰•卡特和凱倫•泰萊交流。

Module 1, Unit 1-6
這幾個單元的事件在倫敦洛維工程公司發生，集中講述洛維工程公司和APU公司面對面開會。

Module 2, Unit 7-11
在這幾個單元裏，各人留在自己的辦公室工作，我們可用電郵、電話和電話會議跟進他們的合併過程。

Module 3, Unit 12-18
同樣，各人留在他們自己的辦公室工作，並以電郵、電話通話和電話會議安排出差悉尼。

Module 4, Unit 19-24
這幾個單元集中講述在倫敦和悉尼召開的視像會議，會上討論合併過程。

Characters 人物

湯姆・菲特

是洛維工程公司的項目經理，他有很多管理轉變的工作經驗，現在他負責協調洛維工程公司和 APU 公司兩個電腦系統的整合。

黛安・甘迺迪

是洛維工程公司的高級經理，是湯姆的直屬上司，黛安負責協助湯姆處理洛維工程公司合併出現的任何難題。她大部份時間和 APU 公司的約翰・卡特一起工作。

約翰・卡特

是 APU 公司的工程和特別項目主管，他要確保在高層方面合併得以順利進行，若出現任何問題，他便需要解決它。

凱倫・泰萊

是 APU 公司的資訊科技總監（CIO），她負責管理APU公司內所有電腦系統，並要確保洛維工程公司的系統將來可以和APU 公司的系統一起使用。

1 Back in the office 回到公司

問候同事 | 描述你的週末 | 解釋現時的活動

Conversation

01
DVD

1 湯姆·菲特星期一上午上班。閱讀以下對話，並觀看短片。他的經理黛安·甘迺迪希望他做甚麼呢？

Tom	**Morning**, Cathy!
Cathy	**Morning**, Tom!
Tom	**Hi**, Julia!
Julia	**Hi**, Tom!
Diane	**Hello**, Tom. **How are you?**
Tom	**Hi, fine, thanks, and you?**
Diane	**Very well, thanks. Good weekend?**
Tom	Yeah, **great, thanks.** We had a children's birthday party for Emily yesterday and ten of her friends came round.
Diane	**Wow!**
Tom	**How was your weekend?**
Diane	**Very busy**, too. At the moment I'm working 24/7 on this APU takeover. So, is everything ready for the presentation today?
Tom	Yes, I think so. Jasmine is making photocopies of your presentation now and I'm just changing something on today's agenda, you know, the lunch at the restaurant.
Diane	Good.
Tom	Tom Field. Oh, hi. Right, OK, thanks! That was Cathy at reception. Jasmine is bringing John Carter and Karen Taylor up to the boardroom now.
Diane	All right! What are we waiting for? Let's go!

Business tip

1 當別人問候你時，你可以重複他們的說話去問候他們：
   Morning, Cathy!   Good afternoon!
   Morning, Tom!   Good afternoon!

2 你只可在星期一問別人週末過得怎樣，但在星期五你可以問他們，接下來的週末有何計劃。

Understanding

01
DVD

2 再看一次，然後回答問題。

   1 Does Tom know Cathy and Julia already?
   2 Did Tom enjoy his weekend?
   3 Who is making photocopies for Tom?
   4 What is Tom doing?
   5 Who telephones Tom?
   6 Where will Tom and Diane meet John Carter and Karen Taylor?

Key phrases

Greeting colleagues	Talking about your weekend
Morning!	Good weekend?
Hi!	Great, thanks!
Hello, … . How are you?	How was your weekend?
Fine, thanks, and you?	Very busy!
Very well!	

Practice

3 配對以下兩部份，組成完整句子。

   1 Hello,   A and you?
   2 How was   B are you?
   3 Very   C Jasmine!
   4 How   D busy!
   5 Fine thanks,   E your weekend?

4 參考 Key phrases 和 Business tip 完成對話。

1 A: _____!　　　　　B: Hello!

2 A: _____?　　　　　B: Great, thanks!

3 A: _____?　　　　　B: Very busy, especially Sunday.

4 A: Good morning!　　　　　　　B: _____!

5 A: _____?　　　　　B: Fine thanks, and you?

01 CD

5 湯姆正和另一位同事羅伯塔對話。將句子排成正確順序完成對話，再聆聽 Track 01 核對答案。

1	Tom	Morning, Roberta.
	Roberta	Great, thanks. I played golf on Sunday. How was your weekend?
	Tom	Fine, thanks. Good weekend?
	Tom	Very nice, thanks.
	Roberta	Morning, Tom. How are you?

Language spotlight

現在進行式用於目前的活動

I'm working 24/7.
Jasmine is making some photocopies.
I'm just changing the agenda.
What are we waiting for?

我們用現在進行式去談及目前在我們附近發生的事。
翻到 158 頁了解更多資料和做練習。

Speaking

6 當你和同事打招呼時，説話熱情和表現愉快非常重要。聆聽 Track 02，然後跟着朗讀這些短語和問題。

02 CD

1 Morning, Cindy!

2 How are you?

3 Fine thanks, and you?

4 Very well!

5 How was your weekend?

6 Great, thanks!

7 現在是星期一早上，你同事歌倫剛放完假回來。在播放錄音前閱讀提示和回應，然後播放 Track 03-04，在叩一聲後説話。再聆聽 Track 04 比較你的對話。

03–04 CD

Colin	Morning!
You	*(Reply.)*
Colin	How are you?
You	*(Say you're fine and ask about him.)*
Colin	Very well, thanks. Good vacation?
You	*(Reply and ask about his vacation.)*
Colin	Very good, thanks. We went to France. What are you working on at the moment?
You	*(Say you're practising your English.)*
Colin	That's a good idea!
You	*(Ask Colin what he's doing.)*
Colin	Oh, I'm waiting for some coffee.

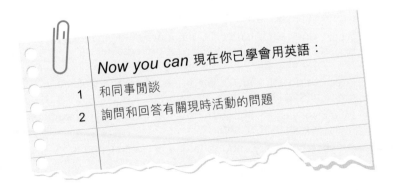

Now you can 現在你已學會用英語：

1 和同事閒談

2 詢問和回答有關現時活動的問題

2   Visitors to the company 來公司的訪客

歡迎公司訪客 | 交換名片 | 描述你的工作

Conversation

02
DVD

1 洛維工程公司的黛安・甘迺迪和湯姆・菲特與 APU 公司的約翰・卡特和凱倫・泰萊見面。閱讀他們的對話並觀看短片。黛安從未見過誰？

Diane	Hello, John! **Good to see you again!**
John	Diane! **Good to see you again, too. Can I introduce you to** Karen Taylor? She's Chief Information Officer at APU.
Diane	**Nice to meet you.**
Karen	**Nice to meet you, too,** Ms Kennedy.
Diane	**Please, call me** Diane. And **let me introduce** you to my colleague, Tom Field. Tom, John is head of engineering and special projects for APU.
Tom	**Pleased to meet you both. Let me give you my card.**
Karen	**Pleased to meet you, too** ... and **here's my card** ...
John	...and mine. So, **what do you do**, Tom?
Tom	Well, I work with Diane a lot! I'm a project manager. I'm responsible for some of the larger projects here at Lowis. And I'm also a change management specialist.
Karen	I see. So do you know many of the different department managers at Lowis?
Tom	I think so, yes. It's important to know the different people and their responsibilities here.
John	Oh yes, that's very important for a project manager.
Diane	Please, have a seat.

Business tip

人們在公司的職銜縮寫通常是這樣：

CEO= Chief Executive Officer 行政總監，是管理這家公司的人。
CFO= Chief Financial Officer 財務總監，是管理公司財務的人。
CIO= Chief Information Officer 資訊總監，是管理公司電腦硬件和軟件的人。

你和訪客説話時，不要用職銜縮寫，因為他們未必明白。提及職銜時總是用全寫。

Understanding

02
DVD

2 再看一次，為每題選取最合適的答案。

1 John has never met
  A Tom.
  B Karen.
  C Diane.

2 Karen Taylor works for
  A a Chief Information Officer.
  B Lowis Engineering.
  C APU.

3 Tom is in charge of
  A Lowis Engineering.
  B large projects in Lowis Engineering.
  C specialists in Lowis Engineering.

Key phrases

Welcoming company guests and exchanging business cards

Good to see you again!	*Let me introduce … .*
Good to see you again, too.	*Pleased to meet you both.*
Can I introduce you to … ?	*Pleased to meet you, too.*
Nice to meet you.	*Let me give you my card.*
Nice to meet you, too.	*Here's my card.*
Please, call me … .	*What do you do?*

Practice

3 配對以下句子。

1 Can I introduce you to Tom?
2 Let me give you my card.
3 What do you do?
4 Nice to meet you, Mr Martinez.
5 Good to see you!

A I'm a computer specialist.
B Good to see you, too.
C Please, call me Carlos.
D Thanks. Here's mine.
E Nice to meet you.

4 從方框選取適合的詞語完成句子。

| at | for | in | of | to | to | too |

1 Pleased _____ meet you, _____.
2 Diane is head _____ personnel _____ Lowis Engineering.
3 I'm responsible _____ the company finances.
4 Can I introduce you _____ Robert?
5 She's a specialist _____ Java programming.

5 使用詞彙完成句子，再聆聽 Track 05 核對答案。

Jasmine   Hi, John / good / see / again /

_____ .

John   Hello, Jasmine / good / see / again / too /

_____ .

Jasmine   Can / introduce / colleague / Julia /

_____ .

John   Pleased / meet / you /

_____ .

Julia   Pleased / meet / too /

_____ .

John   What / do, Julia /

_____ ?

Julia   I / Mr Fisher's / personal assistant /

_____ .

Language spotlight

定期活動使用的一般現在式

She's Chief Information Officer.

What do you do?
I'm responsible for ... .

我們說經常做的事時，會用一般現在式。

翻閱 159 頁了解更多資料和做練習。

Speaking

6 留意以下對話有底線詞彙的重音，再聆聽 Track 06，並朗讀句子。

06

  1 <u>Good</u> to see you again!

     Good to see you again <u>too</u>.

  2 <u>Pleased</u> to meet you both.

     Pleased to meet you <u>too</u>.

  3 <u>Nice</u> to meet you.

     Nice to meet you <u>too</u>.

07–08
CD

7 你和同事湯姆一起拜訪公司的供應商珍妮，在此之前你已認識她。在播放錄音之前閱讀提示和回應。播放 Track 07，然後在嗶一聲後說話，再聆聽 Track 08 比較你的對話。

You	*(Greet Jenny.)*
Jenny	Oh, hello! Good to see you again too! Can I introduce my colleague, Alex?
You	*(Greet Alex.)*
Alex	Nice to meet you too.
You	*(Ask what Alex does.)*
Alex	Oh, I'm responsible for sales and marketing. What about you?
You	*(Tell him your job.)*
Alex	Interesting.
You	*(Introduce your colleague, Tom, to Jenny and Alex.)*
Jenny, Alex, Tom	Hi ... hello ... pleased to meet you both.
You	*(Offer Alex your business card.)*
Alex	Oh, thanks. Here's mine!

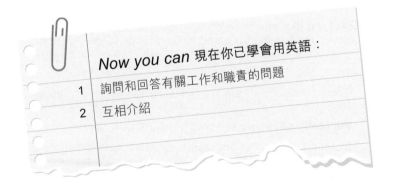

Now you can 現在你已學會用英語：

1 詢問和回答有關工作和職責的問題

2 互相介紹

3 Down to business 直入正題

開始會議 | 提出請求 | 談及將來計劃

Conversation

03
DVD

1 洛維工程公司的黛安•甘廼迪和湯姆•菲特正和 APU 公司的約翰•卡特及凱倫•泰萊開會，會上討論 APU 公司收購洛維的詳情。閱讀他們的對話，並觀看短片。湯姆將會協助誰？

Diane	**So, thank you**, everybody, **for coming to this meeting** today. **Let's start by** discussing what we're going to do over the next few months. John and Karen, you are going to be responsible from the APU side for integrating Lowis into APU.
John	That's right. I'm going to deal with the management side with you and Karen is going to work on systems like IT.
Diane	And **Tom, I want you to** work with Karen.
Tom	OK. How I can help exactly?
Karen	Well, **I'd like you to** help me understand how Lowis works. You're the expert. It's going to be difficult for me to integrate your system into APU without your support.
Tom	That's true.
Diane	Good. I think you're going to find this a very interesting project, Tom.
John	**We really need you to** make this work well, Tom.
Diane	Exactly. Let's look at the current situation at Lowis. Tom, **could you** give John and Karen the handouts while I start the projector?
John	**Would you mind if I** make a quick phone call while you set up?
Diane	Not at all.

Business tip

生意人直接稱呼對方名字是很常見的做法，在英語國家尤其普遍，甚至是第一次見面也可如此。
<u>John</u> and <u>Karen</u>, You're going to be responsible for... .
We really need you to make this work well, <u>Tom</u>.

當你開國際會議時，留心聽別人怎樣講，然後模仿。如果他們直呼名字，你也可直呼別人的名字。

Understanding

03
DVD

2 再看一次，判斷以下句子是正確 T 還是錯誤 F？

1	John and Karen are in charge of integrating Lowis into APU.	T / F
2	Karen deals with HR issues for APU.	T / F
3	Tom knows a lot about APU.	T / F
4	Karen doesn't want Tom's help.	T / F
5	Diane asks Tom to help her.	T / F
6	John doesn't want to make a phone call.	T / F

Key phrases

Starting meetings and making requests

Thank you for coming to this meeting.	*We really need you to ... .*
Let's start by ... +ing	*Could you ...?*
I want you to	*Would you mind if I ...?*
I would / I'd like you to ...	

Practice

3 參考 Key phrases 完成句子。

1 APU _____ like you to start work next week.
2 Would your boss _____ if I change our appointment?
3 I really _____ you to do this for me.
4 Thanks for _____ to this meeting.
5 _____ you send me an email?
6 Let's start _____ talking about the new project.

4 將句裏的詞彙排成正確順序。

1 you / windows / mind / Would / we / open / if / the

_____?

2 boss / needs / him / really / call / you / to / The / give / a

_____.

3 checking / start / information / by / some / Let's

_____.

4 like / to / to / you / come / She'd / meeting / the

_____.

5 reservation / check / you / Could / my

_____?

6 you / for / this / all / coming / morning / to / this / Thank / meeting

_____.

5 想請你同事占士幫你做些事，用自己的資料完成以下請求。

1 James, I want you to ...

_____.

2 Would you mind if I ...

_____?

3 Could you ...

_____?

4 The company really needs you to ...

_____.

5 When that's finished, I'd like you to ...

_____.

Language spotlight

going to 將來式

I'm going to deal with the management side.
It's going to be difficult for me to integrate your systems.
You're going to find this an interesting project.

going to 將來式用於談及未來的計劃、意向或期望。
翻閱 161 頁了解更多資料和做練習。

Speaking

6 going to 這兩個字快讀時連在一起，聽起來很像 gonna，聆聽 Track 09，然後跟着朗讀句子。

09 CD

1 I'm <u>going to</u> phone him.
2 He's <u>going to</u> send an email.
3 What are you <u>going to</u> do?
4 It isn't <u>going to</u> work.
5 Are you <u>going to</u> see him tomorrow?

7 你是項目經理，想請項目成員幫你做事。在播放錄音之前閱讀提示和回應。播放 Track 10，然後在呸一聲後說話，由你先開始。再聆聽 Track 11 比較你的對話。

10–11 CD

You	*(Thank Helen and Colin for coming to the meeting.)*
Helen + Colin	OK, good.
You	*(Ask Helen and Colin to do some things for you.)*
Helen + Colin	Fine. No problem.
You	*(Ask Colin to check the project costs.)*
Colin	Sure. Can I get the figures from you tomorrow morning?
You	*(Say you aren't going to be in the office tomorrow morning. Ask if he can come to your office after the meeting.)*
Colin	Of course.
You	*(Say you'd like Helen to check the factory with you.)*
Helen	Great! When?
You	*(Say you plan to check it on Monday next week.)*
Helen	OK.
You	*(Ask the team to send you all their reports to you by Friday lunch time.)*
Helen + Colin	Sure. No problem.

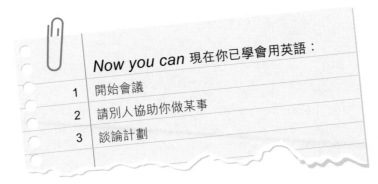

Now you can 現在你已學會用英語：

1 開始會議
2 請別人協助你做某事
3 談論計劃

4　The presentation 匯報

開始匯報 ｜ 匯報次序 ｜ 談及過往

Conversation

04
DVD

1　黛安和湯姆正在向約翰和凱倫報告洛維項目的情況。閱讀他們的對話並觀看短片。洛維在哪些國家設有辦事處？

	OK. So Tom and I **would like to tell you something about** the two biggest projects at Lowis over the last three years: **first**, there's the accounting software - xRoot - that we use for all of our bookkeeping, and **second**, the Jupiter project for the government.
Diane	**So, first of all**, xRoot. Some years ago we used a basic spreadsheet for all of our bookkeeping. This wasn't a problem **then** because we worked in one London office. But **after** we opened offices in Strasbourg, Seoul and then Houston, we realized we needed to upgrade. The system was a problem at first, but we used some consultants to help us and now everything works very well.
Karen	Sorry, do you store your numbers in a Delphic or a Compex database?
Tom	Compex. xRoot only works with Compex.
Diane	Thanks, Tom.
Karen	I see.
Diane	So, **next** topic, Tom can tell you about the Jupiter project.
Tom	Thanks, Diane. Well, I was the project manager for the Jupiter project, which was a £45 ...

Business tip

保持簡潔的匯報結構是個好主意。以下三個步驟是有效的好方法：

1 引言：表達你匯報的主題。

2 主體：提出重點，用資料和數據支持每個重點。

3 結論：總結接收資料後該做甚麼。

Understanding

04
DVD

2 再看一次，為每題選取最合適的答案。

1 In her presentation Diane wants to talk about
   A Lowis offices around the world.
   B APU.
   C two large projects at Lowis.

2 The xRoot system
   A deals with financial figures.
   B deals with sales.
   C deals with office systems.

3 Tom
   A was project manager at xRoot.
   B was the project manager on the Jupiter project.
   C worked for the government.

Key phrases

Giving a presentation	Talking about the past
I would like / I'd like to tell you something about	*After ... , we did ... .*
	Then ... .
First, ... / First of all, ...	
Second, ...	
Third, ...	
Next ...., .	
Finally, ...	

3 配對以下兩部份，組成完整句子。

1	We would like to	A	look at these figures.
2	So, first of all,	B	the project in Turkey, we then … .
3	After we finished	C	six months in Indonesia with … .
4	Then we worked for	D	show you our new product.

4 參考 Key phrases，完成 APU 公司匯報的首段文字。

I would (1) _____ to tell you something about APU: (2) _____, our projects in Southeast Asia, (3) _____, our merger with Lowis Engineering and, thirdly, the Sydney traffic projects.

So, first of (4) _____, Southeast Asia. In 2005 we opened our offices in Jakarta, and Kuala Lumpur in 2007. (5) _____ we started working there, we realized how important it was to have local experts in our team and so we (6) _____ hired graduates from the local universities.

5 用你自己公司的資料，完成以下句子。

1 I would like to tell you something about _____ .
2 Firstly, _____ .
3 Secondly, _____ .
4 So, first of all, _____ .
5 After we _____, we then _____ .

Language spotlight

一般過去式

Some years ago we used Microsoft Excel… .
… we worked in one London office… .
This wasn't a problem then.
I was a project manager… .
… after we opened offices in Strasbourg… .

一般過去式用於談論已完成的活動。
翻到 162 頁了解更多資料和做練習。

Speaking

6 我們在匯報時，常用信號詞如 first 和 second，令觀眾知道快將出現重要資訊。聆聽 Track 12，跟着朗讀短語。

12
CD

  1 First, the costs.

  2 Second, the size.

  3 So, first of all, the new plans.

  4 After that, we closed the company in Ankara.

  5 Then we opened a factory in Malaysia.

7 你要向一群供應商匯報。用以下筆記撰寫匯報，然後聆聽 Track 13 比較你的匯報。

13
CD

Notes

Topic: Payment terms

Want to talk about (1) change in terms (2) reasons for change in terms

Plan: payment terms to change from 60 to 90 days on January 1st.

Reason for change: 90 days is what our customers require.

Now you can 現在你已學會用英語：

  1 開始一個匯報

  2 為匯報排序

  3 談及過往發生的事

5 Questions and answers at the presentation 匯報中的問答

處理問題 | 詢問過往

05
DVD

Conversation

1 黛安和湯姆完成匯報後，約翰和凱倫想問一些有關洛維的問題。閱讀對話並觀看短片。黛安在首爾負責做些甚麼？

Tom	OK, so **do you have any questions?**
John	Yes. Diane, have you always worked here in London?
Diane	**Sorry, I don't understand your question.**
John	Well, I mean did you ever work at any of the Lowis offices outside Britain?
Diane	Ah, I see. **I'm glad you asked that question,** John. Yes, I did. In 2008 I was sales manager responsible for Asia and I worked in Seoul. But I didn't work there for very long, only about six months.
Karen	Were you responsible for the xRoot project in Asia?
Diane	No, I wasn't. That was my boss, Mr Lee Ji-Sung.
John	Ah yes, Mr Lee. I met him last week in Sydney. And how much did the new system cost?
Diane	**That's a good question** ... erm ... **I'm not sure about that.** Tom, do you know?
Tom	Yes. Including the Compex consultants it cost around six million dollars.
Karen	And how long did it take to install?
Tom	That was very fast. The project took nine months.
John	That is fast! **Now I have a question for you, Tom:** when did your work for the Jupiter project start?
Tom:	Oh, **let me think.** It began about 12 months ago when I started work on the ...

Business tip

對匯報結束之後在場參與者發問保持正面態度，這是個好機會讓你重複要點，或提供更多與匯報相關的資料。

Understanding

05
DVD

2 再看一次短片，判斷以下句子是正確 T 還是錯誤 F？

1	Diane has only worked in London.	T / F
2	Diane worked for a short time in Seoul.	T / F
3	Diane's boss wasn't responsible for the xRoot project in Asia.	T / F
4	Tom says the xRoot project cost about six million dollars.	T / F
5	John doesn't think the xRoot project was fast.	T / F

Key phrases

Questions and answers at a presentation

Do you have any questions?	*I'm not sure about that.*
Sorry, I don't understand your question.	*[Now] I have a question for you, Tom.*
I'm glad you asked that question.	*Let me think.*
That's a good question.	

Practice

3 看以下句子，寫出遺漏的字詞。

1 I'm you asked that question. _____
2 Sorry, I don't your question. _____
3 That's a question! _____
4 Have a question for you, Kim. _____
5 Let think. _____

4 將句裏的詞彙排成正確順序。

1 Do / presentation / you / the / any / questions / have / about

_____?

2 not / sure / I'm / about / that / point

_____.

3 question / me / think / Let / about / that

_____.

4 you / question / for / asking / Thank / that

_____.

5 你在這些情況下會説甚麼？

1 you want people to ask you questions after your presentation?

_____

2 you don't understand a question?

_____

3 you aren't sure of the answer to a question?

_____

4 you want some time to think about the answer to a question?

_____

Language spotlight

一般過去式：問題與否定

Were you responsible for the xRoot project?
Did you ever work outside Britain?
I didn't work there long.
No, I wasn't.
How much did the new system cost?

翻到 162 頁了解更多資料和做練習。

Speaking

6 當你問別人問題時，説話的語調非常重要，要讓人知道你在提出問題。
聆聽 Track 14，然後跟着朗讀這些問題。

14
CD

1 How much did it cost?
2 What did you do?
3 How long were you there?
4 Were you the sales manager?
5 When did you arrive?

7 你完成匯報後，你的客戶想問你幾條新產品的問題。用下面資料幫助自己回答問題。在播放錄音前閱讀提示和回應，然後播放 Track 15，在哔一聲後說話。再聆聽 Track 16 比較自己的匯報。

15–16
CD

You	*(Ask if there are questions.)*
Customer 1	Yes. How much time did you need to develop your product?
You	*(Say you don't understand.)*
Customer 1	I mean, how long did it take from start to finish?
You	*(Nine months.)*
Customer 2	Was the product tested in Taiwan?
You	*(Say you aren't certain. Ask if you can send an email with the answer.)*
Customer 2	Of course. How many people worked on the project?
You	*(Say you are glad he asked that question. Say it wasn't many, only six engineers.)*

8 現在代入客戶角色，詢問關於新產品的問題，用以下資料幫助自己提出問題。播放 Track 17，在哔一聲後說話。再聆聽 Track 18 作出比較。

17–18
CD

You	*(Ask if the supplier was responsible for the project.)*
Supplier	Yes, I was.
You	*(Ask how much the project cost.)*
Supplier	I'm afraid I can't tell you that information.
You	*(Say you understand. Ask where the six engineers worked.)*
Supplier	They worked as a team in the UK.
You	*(Say thanks.)*
Supplier	My pleasure.

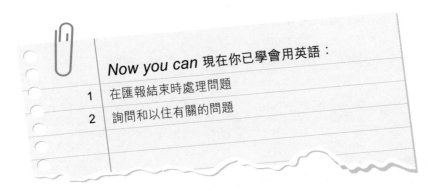

Now you can 現在你已學會用英語：

1 在匯報結束時處理問題

2 詢問和以往有關的問題

6 Closing the meeting 結束會議

結束會議 ｜ 訂立目標 ｜ 提供茶點

Conversation

06
DVD

1 結束會議時，黛安就討論的事作出總結，閱讀他們的對話並觀看短片。
湯姆答應凱倫做甚麼事？

Diane	OK, **let me summarize**: Tom will work with Karen on the integration project full time. Karen will report to John and Tom will report to me.
John	Right, and you and I, Diane, we'll have a meeting or telephone call once a week to check progress.
Diane	Yes.
Tom	OK. So, Karen, I'll make a list of all the IT systems for you so that you know what we have.
Karen	Great! When will you be able to send that to me?
Tom	It'll be on your desk on Wednesday.
Diane	**Are you OK with that**, John?
John	Oh, yes. That's great.
Diane	Good … Well, **I think that's enough for today**.
John	Good.
Diane	Ah, excellent timing. Now, you and I, John, have a factory tour with Chris Fox the production manager in half an hour and since we won't have time for a proper lunch, I ordered some sandwiches for us all.
John	Thank you.
Karen	Good idea.
Diane	So, **help yourself to something**.

Karen	Thank you.
John	Looks good.
Diane	Tom, **could you pass me** a bottle of water?
Karen	**Sorry, is that chicken? I'm afraid I don't eat meat.**
Tom	Oh, sorry. **Would you like some of these** sandwiches? Cheese, egg and ... I think those ones are salad sandwiches.
Karen	I think I'll just have some fruit, thanks.
Diane	Good idea. **Have some** of this mango. **It's delicious!**

Business tip

你為客人提供食物或飲品時，要留心他們有無特別要求，他們可能不吃某幾類食物，故要在提供飲食之前詢問清楚。

Understanding

06
DVD

2 再看一次短片，改正每句內的錯處。

1 Tom and Karen will work on the integration project part time. _____

2 John and Diane will have a meeting every month. _____

3 On Friday Tom will send the list of IT systems to Karen. _____

4 Diane ordered some pizzas for lunch. _____

5 Karen doesn't eat fruit. _____

Key phrases

1 Finishing a meeting

Let me summarize:	*I think that's enough for today.*
Are you OK with that?	

2 Refreshments

Help yourself to something.	*Would you like some ...?*
Could you pass me ... ?	*Have some ... .*
Sorry, is that chicken?	*It's delicious.*
I'm afraid I don't eat meat.	

Practice

3 配對以下兩部份，組成完整句子。

1 Let me summarize   A bottle of water?

2 Would you like a   B OK with that?

3 Are you   C our meeting.

4 I'm afraid   D sandwiches.

5 Have some   E I can't eat nuts.

4 使用詞彙完成句子。

1 think / enough / today _____.

2 Please / yourself / something / eat _____.

3 Could / pass / orange juice / John? _____?

4 Would / like some / fruit _____?

5 按對話的第二部分，完成第一部份。

1 A _____

   B A mineral water? Here you are!

2 A _____

   B Yes, that's fine for me and my company.

3 A _____

   B Some cheese? Oh yes, thanks very much.

4 A _____

   B No problem. We can order some vegetarian food.

5 A _____

   B Mmm, you're right! The mango is delicious!

Language spotlight

will 一般將來式

It'll be on your desk… [承諾]
We won't have time… [預期]
Tom will work with Karen. [指示]
Karen will report to John. [指示]
When will you be able to send…? [指示]
will 用於承諾、預期某事或給予指示。

翻到 163 頁了解更多資料和做練習。

Speaking

6 説話時，我們通常會縮寫 *will*。聆聽 Track 19，跟着朗讀例子。

(19 CD)

1 It'll cost a lot of money.

2 What'll he do?

3 She won't be at the meeting.

4 Tom'll finish the report tomorrow.

5 When'll he call her?

6 They'll fly back tomorrow.

7 會議結束後，你請來自美國的同事仙迪吃茶點。用以下的資料幫助自己和她對話。在播放錄音前閱讀提示和回應，然後播放 Track 20，在呸一聲後説話，再聆聽 Track 21 比較你的對話。

(20–21 CD)

You *(Say that's the end of the meeting.)*

Cindy That's good.

You *(Say you ordered some refreshments. You hope Cindy is hungry!)*

Cindy Yes. Very.

You *(Tell her to help herself.)*

Cindy Mmm, it looks great!

You *(Ask her to pass you an orange juice.)*

Cindy Here you are. Um … is that beef in the sandwich? I'm afraid I don't eat meat!

You *(Offer her some cheese salad sandwiches.)*

Cindy Oh thanks! Sorry to be difficult!

You *(No problem. Tell her you can't eat fish.)*

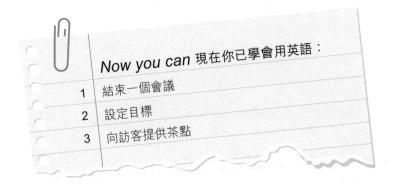

Now you can 現在你已學會用英語：

1 結束一個會議

2 設定目標

3 向訪客提供茶點

7   On the phone to Australia 打電話到澳洲

打電話給生意伙伴 │ 打電話找某人

Telephone call

1 湯姆打電話到澳洲找凱倫。聆聽 Track 22 的電話對話。為何湯姆找不到
在悉尼的凱倫？

22
CD

1	Kim	**Kim Benders speaking**.
	Tom	**Hello, this is** Tom Field **from** Lowis Engineering in London. **Can I speak to Karen Taylor, please?**
	Kim	Oh hello, Mr Field. I'm Karen's assistant. **I'm afraid she's not in the office** today. **She's on a business trip to** Malaysia. **Can I help you?**
	Tom	Oh, I see. Well, **can you put me through to** John Carter?
	Karen	Of course. **Hold the line, please**. Hello, Mr Field? **I'm sorry but his line's busy at the moment. Can I take a message**?
	Tom	No, don't worry. **I'll call him back later**.
	Kim	By the way, I know that Karen checks her emails every evening.
	Tom	Yes, that's a good idea. **I'll send her an email. Thanks for your help**.
	Kim	And she'll be back in the office on Friday, so you can speak to her then.
	Tom	OK. Good to know. Thanks a lot.
	Kim	No worries.
	Tim	Goodbye!
	Kim	Bye!

Business tip

Thanks for your help.

和其他公司的經理秘書或助手説話時，總要記得感謝他們。他們會記得你是個友善的生意伙伴，在你將來找他們的經理時，他們會更樂意協助你。

Understanding

22
CD

2 再聽一次，然後為每題選出最合適的答案。

1 Kim Benders
   A works for Lowis Engineering.
   B is Karen's boss.
   C works for Karen.

2 John is
   A in Malaysia.
   B speaking on the phone.
   C in a meeting.

3 Tom wants
   A Kim to tell John to telephone him.
   B Kim to tell John he telephoned.
   C to telephone John later.

4 Tom decides to
   A write to Karen.
   B telephone Karen later.
   C visit Karen.

Key phrases

Telephoning

Calling a business partner	Answering the phone
Hello, this is Tom Field from … .	*Kim Benders speaking.*
Can I speak to Karen Taylor, please?	*I'm afraid she's not in the office.*
Can you put me through to … ?	*She's on a business trip to … .*
I'll call back later.	*Can I help you?*
I'll send her an email.	*Hold the line, please.*
Thanks for your help.	*I'm sorry but his line's busy at the moment.*
	Can I take a message?

Practice

3 配對以下兩部份，組成完整句子。

1	Hold	A	take a message?
2	Can I	B	back later.
3	I'll call	C	for your help.
4	Thanks	D	speaking.
5	David Knopf	E	the line, please.

4 將句裏的詞彙排成正確順序。

1 you / please / put / through / me / to / Can / Julia,

_____?

2 afraid / meeting / he's / I'm / in / a / at / moment / the

_____.

3 I / Jasmine / speak / Goodman, / to / Can / please

_____?

4 him / write / an / I'll / email

_____.

5 Knopf / this / xRoot / Software / is / David / Hi, / from

_____.

5 你遇到這些情況會說甚麼？

1 The telephone rings and you answer.

_____

2 The caller wants to speak to your manager. She's in a meeting.

_____

3 You want the caller to wait while you transfer their call to somebody else.

_____

4 You have to tell the caller that the person they want is speaking on the phone.

_____

5 You offer to take a message.

_____

Language spotlight

短語動詞

Well, can you <u>put</u> me <u>through</u> to John Carter?
I'll <u>call</u> him <u>back</u> later.

翻閱 164 頁了解更多短語動詞的資料和做練習。

Speaking

6 當你想別人幫你做事時，在句尾加 please，這樣可幫你達到目的。聆聽 Track 23，跟着朗讀以下句子。

(CD 23)

1 Can I speak to Karen Taylor, please?
2 Can you put me through to Susie Goh, please?
3 Can you take a message, please?
4 Hold the line, please.

7 你需要打電話給你在美國的供應商蓋普。在播放錄音前閱讀提示和回應，然後播放 Track 24，在呠一聲後説話，再聆聽 Track 25 比較你的對話。

(CD 24–25)

Jodie Compex Incorporated, Jodie King speaking. How can I help you?

You *(Give your name and your company name and ask to speak to Frank Linker.)*

Jodie I'm afraid he's in a meeting.

You *(Say you'll send him an email. Then ask to be put through to Susie Goh.)*

Jodie I'm sorry but her line's busy at the moment. Can I take a message?

You *(Tell her not to worry and you'll call back later. End the call politely.)*

Jodie Goodbye!

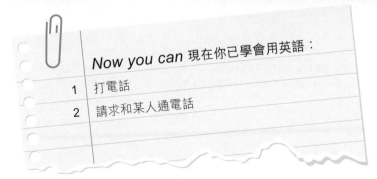

Now you can 現在你已學會用英語：

1 打電話

2 請求和某人通電話

8 Emailing Australia 電郵到澳洲

提出建議 | 提出預約 | 設定不在辦公室的自動電郵回覆

Email

1 湯姆發了電郵給凱倫。湯姆提議了甚麼？

Dear Karen

I tried to call you today **but** I heard you are on a business trip.

With regard to your email and your questions, **I think it's a good idea if** we discuss them with Diane, John and some other people from Lowis. **I suggest that** I organize a telephone conference call on Friday at 8 am UK time (6 pm in Australia). Your assistant said you'll be back in the office then. **Could you let me know if that's convenient for you?**

I look forward to speaking to you soon.

Best wishes
Tom

I am out of the office until Thursday 7th November. I will be back in the office on Friday 8th November. I will be reading my emails every evening.

Thanks, Karen

Business tip

Dear Karen
電郵開首雖然可以有各種不同方式，但商業電郵通常用 Dear... 。其他方式如 Hello Karen、Hi Karen、Karen 等，顯得太不正式。此外，只在認識對方的情況下才會直呼其名。

Understanding

2 再讀一次電郵，判斷以下句子是正確 (T) 還是錯誤 (F) ?

1	Tom spoke to Karen.	T / F
2	Karen isn't on a business trip.	T / F
3	Diane wants to organize a telephone conference call.	T / F
4	Karen is back in the office on Thursday.	T / F
5	Karen is reading her emails on her business trip.	T / F

Key phrases

Business emails

1 Business emails	2 Making suggestions and appointments
I tried to call you ... but	
With regard to	I think it's a good idea if ... .
I look forward to speaking to you soon.	I suggest that I ... .
Best wishes	Could you let me know if that's convenient for you?

3 Automated replied

I am out of the office [in ...] until ... .

Practice

3 從方框找出每題遺漏的字詞，完成句子。

a   but   me   until   we   your

1 With regard to project in India ....

_____

2 I think it's good idea if we ...

_____

3 I tried to speak to you this morning you were in a meeting.

_____

4   I suggest that meet as soon as possible.

_____

5   Could you let know if that's convenient?

_____

6   I'm out of the office Monday.

_____

4   這封是給黛安的助理茉莉·歌文的電郵，將每句排成正確順序。

Dear Ms Goodman

_____ : Best wishes

_____ : With regard to our meeting tomorrow, ...

_____ : I look forward to seeing you tomorrow.

_____ : I suggest that I invite our accountant, Gordon King, to the meeting.

__1__ : I tried to call you this afternoon but you were in a meeting.

_____ : I think it's a good idea if we also discuss the project costs.

Priti Makesch

5   你正在寫電郵給一個生意伙伴，用自己的資料完成電郵。

Dear _____

(1) _____ I tried to call you (2) _____

but your assistant said you are (3) _____ .

With regard to your (4) _____ I think it's a good idea if I

(5) _____. Also, I suggest that I (6) _____ .

Could you let me know if that's convenient for you?

Best wishes

(7) _____

Language spotlight

in / on / at 時間介詞

*I suggest that I organize a telephone conference **on** Friday **at** 8 am.*

*I will be back in the office **on** Friday 8ᵗʰ November.*
我們會：
月份和年份用 In：In July / In 1989
星期和日期用 On：On Friday / On May 30th
時間和節日用 At：At eight o'clock / At Christmas

翻閱 165 頁複習時間介詞和做練習。

Writing

6 一個重要的美國客人在你的留言信箱留言，問了幾個關於你公司的產品和服務的問題。你嘗試打電話給她，但她到了中國出差。發一封電郵給她，說你想和她聯絡，提議明天北京時間下午六時打電話給她，並詢問她酒店的電話號碼。

7 替自己下星期寫一封不在辦公室的自動電郵回覆。你下星期整個星期都放假，而你的助理蘇珊・史密夫可用她的電郵 smith@XYZ.com 處理查詢。

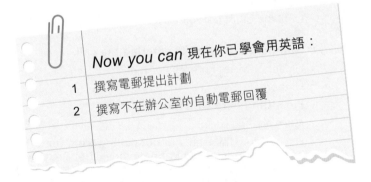

Now you can 現在你已學會用英語：

| 1 | 撰寫電郵提出計劃 |
| 2 | 撰寫不在辦公室的自動電郵回覆 |

9 Starting the telephone conference call
開始電話會議

參與電話會議（telco） | 和其他與會者打招呼

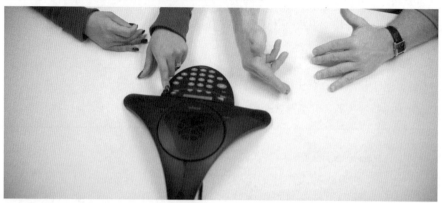

Telephone conference call

1 湯姆、黛安、約翰、凱倫和羅拔正在參與電話會議。聆聽 Track 26 的對話。湯姆在哪裏？

26
CD

Recorded voice	**Welcome to the Maxtime telephone conference service. Please enter your conference call PIN followed by the pound sign. Please give your name.**
Tom	Tom Field.
Recorded voice	Until the other participants arrive, you will hear some music.
Recorded voice	**Another participant is entering the call.**
John	Hi, John Carter here. Hello, Tom?
Tom	Hi there.
John	**I'm sitting here with Karen.**
Karen	Morning, Tom.
Tom	Hello, Karen, hi John. **I'm not calling from the office** because **I'm working at home** today. But Diane **will call in in a minute**, together with Robert Holden. You want to ask him about the xRoot systems for the accounting department.
Recorded voice	Another participant is entering the call.
Diane	Hello. Diane and Robert here.
Robert	Hi, everybody. **Sorry we're late**.
Tom	No problem. **Well, let's start**. Karen, you have some questions for Robert and me, I think.

Karen	Yes, thanks Tom. Robert, **can you tell me** how many different IT systems you need for the financial accounts for Lowis?
Robert	Hmm, we use three systems.
Karen	Yes, but **why do you have** three IT systems?
Robert	Because Lowis is an international company. One system is for the local figures in each country – the US, Korea or Germany. The second system collects the figures from all over the world. The third system prepares the figures for our management and the tax office.
Karen	And how much time does the process need?
Robert	Not much. We can prepare the complete annual report in two days.
John	Yes, that is good. Tell me, Robert, **how many** people work in the accounts department?
Robert	Only a few. Including the trainees it's ... erm ... fifteen.
Karen	Right. Tom, can you tell me **how much** space the company computer servers need?
Tom	Only a little. We have them all in the basement. Maybe five square metres.
John	I see, Diane, what do you think about ... ?

Business tip

在電話會議裏，總要留心聽別人的話，讓他們説完要説的話。如果兩個人同時説話，沒有人可以理解對方。

Understanding

26
CD

2 再聽一次，回答以下問題。

1 Why is Tom not in the office?

2 Why does Lowis have three IT systems for the accounting department?

3 How long does it take to do the figures for Lowis?

Key phrases

Starting telcos	Asking questions
Tom here.	*Can you tell me ... ?*
I'm sitting here with Karen.	*Why do you have ... ?*
I'm calling from home.	*How much ... ?*
I'm working at home today.	*How many ... ?*
Diane will call in in a minute.	
Sorry we're late.	
Let's start.	

3 配對以下兩部份，組成完整句子。

1	Sorry	A	computers do we need?
2	Let's	B	what you know about the software?
3	I'm working	C	start with the agenda.
4	Ken will call in	D	time do we need for the meeting?
5	Can you tell me	E	later.
6	How much	F	I'm late.
7	How many	G	from home today.

4 將句裏的詞彙排成正確順序。

1 Mondays / home / Diane / from / on / works _____ .

2 sitting / Bernadette / here / with / I'm / Kim / and _____ .

3 you / costs / much / tell / Can / how / it / me _____ ?

4 you / many / know / worldwide / how / offices / you /
  have / Do _____ ?

5 約翰和凱倫正與韓國供應商朴先生開另一次電話會議。將句子排成正確順序以完成對話，再聆聽 Track 27 核對答案。

1	John	John Carter here. Hello, Mr Park.
	Mr Park	No problem, Ms Taylor.
	John	My colleague Karen Taylor will call in in a moment from home.
	John	Good. Well, let's start. Can you tell us how much time you have for us today?
	Karen	Hello, John. Hello, Mr Park. Sorry I'm late.
	Mr Park	As much time as you want, Mr Carter.
	John	Great! Well, first of all, we need to know how much your new products will cost?
	Mr Park	Good evening, Mr Carter.

Language spotlight

How much / How many / a little / a few

我們用 much 表示不可數事物（例如：How much space do we have?），而用 many 表示可數事物（例如：How many computers do we have?）。

回答 How much 的提問時，用 a little（例如：We only have a little space.），回答 How many 的提問時，則用 a few（例如：We only have a few computers.）。

翻閱 166 頁參考更多例子和做練習。

Speaking

6 練習以下的問句形式，聆聽並跟着朗讀句子。

28
CD

1 How much does it cost?
2 Can you tell me when she'll call in?
3 How many offices do you have?
4 Why do you have so many systems?

29–30
CD

7 你正和在東京的渡邊純和在巴黎的柏斯高·本諾開電話會議，討論你們一起參與的工作項目。在播放錄音前閱讀提示和回應，然後播放 Track 29，在嗶一聲後説話。再聆聽 Track 30 比較你的對話。

Recorded voice	Another caller is entering the conference.
You	*(Say hello and give your name.)*
Jun + Pascale	Hi, Jun here. Hello, this is Pascale!
You	*(Apologize for being late.)*
Pascale	That's OK!
You	*(Say you're working from your home. Then ask how much time we need for the telco.)*
Jun	As much time as you want. Well, let's start. Can you tell us how many people you have for this project in your office?
You	*(Only a few. Ask Pascale how many people she has.)*
Pascale	Oh, it's the same for me. Only a few.
You	*(Ask Pascale how many people she needs.)*
Pascale	I think another five at least!

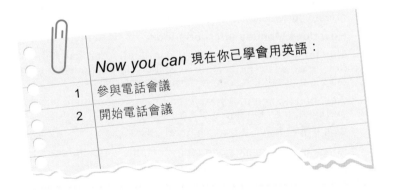

Now you can 現在你已學會用英語：

1 參與電話會議
2 開始電話會議

10 Ending the telephone conference call
結束電話會議

商討安排 | 在電話說"再見" | 談及定好的計劃

Telephone conference call

1 湯姆、黛安、約翰、凱倫和羅拔正在參與電話會議。聆聽 Track 31 的對話。湯姆會在樸茨茅斯逗留多少晚？

Diane	... and then we can integrate our computer system with yours and cut the number of computer servers.
Robert	And that cuts the costs, of course.
John	Yes, that's very important. Do you agree, Karen?
Karen	Yes, definitely. By the way Tom, **I just want to let you know** that I'm flying to London next week. Can we have a meeting some time? **What are your plans on** Monday?
Tom	**Let me check my schedule for next week**. Well, on Monday morning I'm having a meeting with the sales team to talk about your Customer Relationship Management tool.
Karen	**How does Monday afternoon look**?
Tom	Mm, **let me take a look**. Sorry, not good. After that, I'm driving down to Portsmouth to visit our largest customer and tell them about the company changes.
Karen	Well, can I come with you? Then I have a chance to see you and meet the customers of Lowis Engineering.
Tom	Well, I'm not sure if that's a good idea.
Diane	I think that's a really good idea, Tom. It's very important for Karen to meet our customers as soon as possible.
Tom	Yes, of course. It's just that I'm staying in Portsmouth on Monday night and I'm not driving back to London until Tuesday night.

Karen	No problem, Tom. I can take a train on Tuesday morning.
John	Excellent. That's a good solution, I think. Now, I have another meeting I'm afraid ...
Diane	Me too. **Good to speak to you**, John ... Karen.
Karen	Great! **Speak to you soon**, Diane and Robert. **Nice speaking to you**, Tom. See you on Monday.
Tom	Right, Monday then. **I'm looking forward to it**, Karen.

Business tip

Great! Excellent!
當你同意你的生意伙伴的看法，你可以用這些正面的詞彙，增進彼此關係。

Understanding

2 再聽一次，判斷以下句子是正確 T 還是錯誤 F？

31
CD

1	Karen is flying to London tomorrow.	T / F
2	Tom is busy all day on Monday.	T / F
3	Tom is visiting a supplier in Portsmouth.	T / F
4	Tom likes the idea of Karen going with him to Portsmouth.	T / F
5	Karen will catch a train back to London on Tuesday.	T / F

Key phrases

1 Making arrangements	2 Saying 'goodbye'
I just want to let you know	*Good to speak to you, ...*
What are your plans on ...?	*Speak to you soon.*
Let me check my schedule for next week.	*Nice speaking to you, ...*
How does Monday afternoon look?	*I'm looking forward to it.*
Let me take a look.	

Practice

3 用方框的詞語完成句子。

> lunchtime   Mr Carter's   seeing   speak   Tuesday

1 _____ to you soon.
2 How does Thursday _____ look?
3 Let me check _____ schedule for next week.

4 I'm looking forward to _____ you.

5 What are your plans on _____?

4 配對以下句子。

1	How does Saturday look?	**A**	Well, I'll go to work and finish the report.
2	What are your plans on Monday?	**B**	February? Let me check my calendar.
3	What about next month?	**C**	Yes, I think it should be a good meeting.
4	I'm looking forward to it!	**D**	Oh, I never do business on the weekend!

5 閱讀以下約翰和韓國供應商朴先生的對話。從每題找出至少一個錯處並更正它。

1 J   I just want to let you know. I'm flying to Seoul last week.

_____

2 P   Oh, let my check me schedule.

_____

3 J   How do Wednesday look?

_____

4 P   Hmm, not too bad. What about on ten o'clock in your hotel?

_____

5 J   That's fine. I'm have a meeting at the APU office after lunch.

_____

6 P   OK. So, ten o'clock on Wednesday. Nice speaking at you, John.

_____

7 J   Yes. He's looking forward to seeing you soon!

_____

Language spotlight

用現在進行式談及將來

On Monday morning I'm having a meeting.
I'm staying in Portsmouth on Monday night.
I'm not driving back until Tuesday night.

我們可以用現在進行式談及一些已計劃、安排妥當和取得同意的未來活動。

翻閱 159 頁參考更多例子和做練習。

Speaking

6 當你和別人在電話上說再見時，表現熱情和友善很重要。如果可以的話，可稱呼對方的名字。聆聽 Track 32，並跟着朗讀句子。

32
CD

1 Good to speak to you, Linda! Bye!
2 Speak to you soon, Kim!
3 Nice speaking to you, Ms Carter. Goodbye!
4 I'm looking forward to it, Pascale. Bye!
5 Well, goodbye then, Alex!

7 你正和在日本的渡邊純進行電話會議，討論一個你們合作的項目，並安排一次會面。在播放錄音前閱讀提示和回應，然後播放 Track 33，在嗶一聲後說話。再聆聽 Track 34 比較你的對話。

33–34
CD

Jun   Well, I think a meeting is a very good idea.
You   *(Say you are flying to Tokyo next week.)*
Jun   Let me check the schedule.
You   *(Ask about Tuesday afternoon.)*
Jun   Oh, I'm sorry, I'm visiting a supplier outside Tokyo on Tuesday.
You   *(Say you're staying in Tokyo until Friday.)*
Jun   Oh, very good. Then I have a chance to see you on Thursday morning.
You   *(Say you are meeting somebody at your hotel in the morning. Ask about his plans for Thursday afternoon.)*
Jun   Yes, that's fine. Is three o'clock OK?
You   *(Say that's an excellent idea.)*
Jun   Great. Well, it was good to speak to you, Karl. See you next week!
You   *(Say you're looking forward to it and goodbye.)*
Jun   Goodbye!

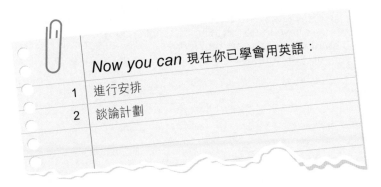

Now you can 現在你已學會用英語：

1 進行安排
2 談論計劃

11 Making plans by email 通過電郵商定計劃

提出請求及建議 | 談及不允許發生的事

Email

1 凱倫發了一封電郵給湯姆。閱讀電郵。她提出了甚麼建議？

Dear Tom

Following our telco discussion this afternoon, I had an idea. **Why don't I come to your meeting on Monday morning with the Lowis sales team?**

If this is OK for you, we can show your sales people the APU Customer Relationship Management system together. We must make sure they are happy about using it. Then **perhaps we could** all have lunch together before driving down to Portsmouth in the afternoon. **How do you feel about this?**

By the way, I'm going to take the train back to London on Monday night, after the meeting in Portsmouth. I have an appointment with Peter King from the Lowis legal department on Tuesday morning and I mustn't be late for that. John also says I have to check the servers in London as soon as possible. But I don't have to do anything else until Friday when I fly back to Sydney, so **shall we** meet again on Wednesday morning? If that's suitable for you, **do you think you could** reserve a meeting room in the office for us?

Best regards

Karen

Business tip

We must make sure...

如果想你同事同意做某事，可以用 we 而不用 you 或 I，因這樣讓他們覺得大家正在一起做這事。

Understanding

2 再讀一次電郵，在每題找出一個錯處，然後更正。

1 John wants to come to Tom's meeting.
2 The salespeople already use the APU system.
3 Tom and Karen are taking the train to Portsmouth.
4 Karen must meet Diane Kennedy on Tuesday morning.
5 Karen mustn't check the servers for John.
6 Karen doesn't have to fly back to Sydney on Friday.

Key phrases

Making suggestions	Requests and asking for opinions
Why don't I ... ?	*How do you feel about this? / What's your opinion on ...?*
If this is OK for you, ...	
Perhaps we could	*Shall we ...?*
	Do you think you could ... ? / Would you mind + ing ... ?

Practice

3 配對以下兩部份，組成完整句子。

1 How do you feel
2 What's your opinion
3 Shall we
4 Would you
5 Perhaps we

A mind booking me a flight?
B have a meeting next week?
C on this?
D could speak to Diane about this.
E about this issue?

4 將句裏的詞語排成正確順序。

1 to / you / and / mind / speaking / Jun / Would / Pascale

_____?

2 your / the / on / opinion / problem / What's

_____?

3 think / you / could / you / send / me / report / the / Do

_____?

4 send / the / the / figures / to / we / project / Shall / manager

_____?

5 this / for / is / OK / you / If, / we / work / together / can

_____.

6 don't / meeting / have / we / a / on / Why / Wednesday

_____?

5 參考 48 頁完成以下電郵。

Dear John

Following our meeting this morning, I spoke to my manager, Mr Lee.
I think it would be helpful if we had a telco to discuss your ideas.
(1) _____ I arrange a telco for next Friday morning?
Perhaps
(2) _____ talk about the prices together.
How (3) _____ idea?

If (4) _____ you, we can also find a time for you to visit
our factory. You (5) _____ see how we make our motors,
it's very impressive!

Would (6) _____ emailing me to say if Friday is OK?
Many thanks

Best regards

Keow

Language spotlight

表示義務的情態詞

We <u>must</u> make sure = 這對我非常重要，而且是百分之一百需要的。
I <u>mustn't</u> be late = 這事不能發生，對我非常重要。
John says <u>I have to</u> check = 對其他人來説，這事的發生非常重要。
<u>I don't have to</u> fly back to Sydney until Friday = 這事並非必要。

翻閱 166 頁了解更多資料和做練習。

Writing

6 你想探訪你在巴黎的同事柏斯高 • 本諾。用以下筆記寫一封電郵。

- Say you are visiting Paris next week for a sales conference.
- Suggest you visit Pascale to discuss the project progress.
- Suggest you take her to lunch.
- Ask how she feels about this.
- Suggest you meet her at one o'clock at her office.
- Ask if she can make reservations in a restaurant.

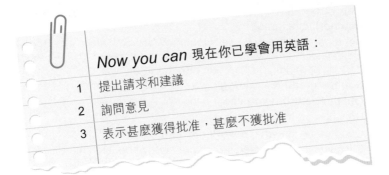

Now you can 現在你已學會用英語：

1	提出請求和建議
2	詢問意見
3	表示甚麼獲得批准，甚麼不獲批准

12 Telephone small talk 電話閒談

電話閒談 | 提出建議 | 商定安排

Telephone call

1 約翰·卡特打電話給倫敦的湯姆·菲特。聆聽 Track 35 的對話，約翰的提議是甚麼？

Tom	Tom Field.
John	Hi Tom, John here.
Tom	Well, good morning … sorry, good afternoon, John. **How's the weather** there today?
John	Hot today and the radio says tomorrow will be hotter! My sons want me to take them down to the beach over the weekend so they can do a bit of surfing and we can have a barbecue.
Tom	**Sounds great! It's raining** here in London right now.
John	**Oh, too bad! Did you see** the football last night?
Tom	No, I missed it.
John	Good game. So **what's work like at the moment**?
Tom	Difficult! Not all the teams here are happy about the merger. And I think the legal department will be even more difficult. But Karen is going to talk to their boss, Peter King, soon.
John	Right. Umm. Tom, **I was wondering if you could** visit our offices here in Sydney? You could stay for a week and meet the people here.
Tom	Er …well, yes, but have you spoken to Diane about it?
John	Not yet. She's not in the office at the moment. I'll call her again later.
Tom	I see. Well, …
John	So, **when is a good time for you**?
Tom	Oh, well, **I have to check my schedule** first. I'll send an email with some suggestions. Is that OK?
John	Yes, that's fine and I have to speak to Diane. Good. Well, **what are you doing this weekend?** Are you doing anything … ?

Business tip

How's the weather there today?

和生意伙伴閒談以建立友好關係，在許多文化裏都是個好的做法，就算只是打電話問候對方也是好的。閒談指說一些日常話題如天氣、運動或工作。這樣做很重要，因為人們愛與他們喜歡的人做生意。

Understanding

35
CD

2 再聽一次，選取最合適的答案。

1 Tom

   A has some problems with the merger.

   B doesn't have much work to do.

   C is going to a meeting.

2 John wants

   A to visit Lowis.

   B Tom to visit APU.

   C Tom to move to Sydney.

3 John

   A has written to Diane about Tom's proposed visit.

   B has spoken to Diane about Tom's proposed visit.

   C is going to speak to Diane about Tom's proposed visit.

Key phrases

1 Telephone small talk

How's the weather ... ?	*What are your plans for this weekend?*
What's work like at the moment?	*It's raining here.*
Did you see the football / tennis / basketball last night?	*Sounds great.*
	Too bad.
What are you doing this weekend?	

2 Making suggestions and arrangements

I was wondering if you could	*I have to check my schedule.*
When is a good time for you?	

Practice

3 參考 Key phrases 完成句子。

1 _____ your plans for next week?

2 _____ my schedule for Friday.

3 _____ see Pascale's presentation yesterday?

4 _____ could send me the figures.

5 _____ time for you to see me?

4 完成説話者A的句子。

1. **A:** It's _____ .
   B: Really? It's raining here as well.

2. **A:** _____ you _____?
   B: For this evening? I'm going to the movies.

3. **A:** _____ at the moment?
   B: Terrible. We don't have enough people for all the work.

4. **A:** Did _____ last night?
   B: The football? No, I missed it.

5. **A:** _____? Thursday 2.00 pm?
   B: Thursday afternoon is great.

5 凱倫打電話給洛維法律部的彼得・金安排預約。將句子排成正確順序以完成對話，然後聆聽 Track 36 核對答案。

1	Karen	How's the weather in London?
	Peter	Hmm, I have to check my schedule. Oh, I'm sorry but the afternoon's no good.
	Peter	Well, on Tuesday perhaps.
	Karen	Sure. When's a good time for you? The afternoon, maybe?
	Peter	It's raining here.
	Karen	Well, what are you doing on Tuesday morning?
	Karen	Too bad! Listen, I'm visiting the UK next week. I was wondering if we could have a meeting some time?
	Peter	Tuesday morning is fine.

Language spotlight

比較級

Hot – hotter

Difficult – more difficult

比較級用於比較不同的人或事，如 hot 加 -er 變成 hotter。較長的詞如 difficult，加 more 變成 more difficult。

翻到 168 頁了解更多資料和做練習。

Speaking

37
CD

6 你在句子裏説 have 時，後面的 to 不會讀成重音。聆聽 Track 37，然後跟着朗讀這些句子。

1 I <u>have to</u> check my schedule.
2 She doesn't <u>have to</u> come.
3 He <u>has to</u> be on time.
4 I <u>have to</u> phone.
5 We don't <u>have to</u> do anything.
6 It <u>has to</u> work first time.

38–39
CD

7 你打電話給曼徹斯特的同事歌倫。在播放錄音前閱讀提示和回應，然後播放 Track 38，在嗶一聲後説話，你先開始。再聆聽 Track 39 比較你的對話。

You *(Say hello and ask about the weather.)*
Colin Oh, hello! It's raining here!
You *(Reply. Ask about his work.)*
Colin Very busy!
You *(Say you are visiting Manchester next week and ask if you can visit him.)*
Colin Well, next week is busy, but I'm sure it's possible.
You *(Ask what he's planning for Thursday.)*
Colin Hmm, not so good. What are you doing on Wednesday?
You *(Say you need to check your schedule.)*
Colin No problem.
You *(Ask when on Wednesday is good.)*
Colin Wednesday morning is fine.

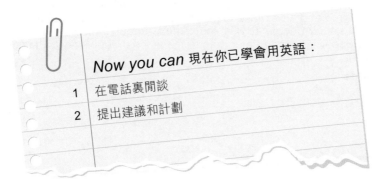

Now you can 現在你已學會用英語：

1 在電話裏閒談
2 提出建議和計劃

13 Arranging the business trip 安排出差

寫商業電郵安排出差 ｜ 請你的同事協助做某事

1 閱讀湯姆．菲特發給約翰的電郵及約翰的回信。湯姆計劃在悉尼逗留多少晚？

Dear John

Following our phone call this morning, I have looked at my schedule and **the week starting** Monday October 20 is a good time for me to visit the APU offices in Sydney.

If you are happy with that, I'll arrive from London on the Friday before. **Would it be possible for** APU **to** book me a room in a hotel from October 17–24? I will fly back to London on October 25.

Regarding the agenda for our discussions, I could arrange a conference call with us three and also Diane to make a list of important topics. If you want, I'll invite other people as well, for example Robert Holden from the accounting department and Peter King from the legal department. **Please let me know.**

Best regards

Tom

Dear Tom

Thanks for your email. Yes, the dates are fine and we look forward to seeing you then. I think a telco in advance to agree your agenda with Diane is a good idea, but I don't think it's necessary to involve Robert and Peter at the moment. After the telco, Karen will set up some meetings with the relevant people here.

My assistant - Pia Levene - will organize your accommodation and she'll email you soon. By the way, would you like to do something on the Saturday evening? Maybe a harbour cruise and dinner? **Let me know if that's OK for you.**

Best wishes

John

Business tip

用英文寫電郵給同事或伙伴時，確保寄出之前花點時間檢查它。甚至找別人幫你檢查一次將會更好。

Understanding

2 再讀一次兩封電郵，回答以下問題。

1 What does Tom want APU to do?
2 What two things does Tom suggest?
3 What does John think about Tom's two suggestions?
4 Who will reserve Tom a hotel room?
5 What invitation does John make?

Key phrases

1 Emailing to make arrangements

Following our phone call … .	*Please let me know.*
Thanks for your email.	*Let me know if that's … .*
The week starting / ending … .	*Best regards / wishes, … .*
Regarding … . / As regards … .	

2 Asking for support / help

Would it be possible for … to … ?

Practice

3 在方框選取合適的詞完成句子。

as   ending   for [x2]   if

1 Thanks very much _____ your email.
2 Let me know _____ that's OK.
3 _____ regards the meeting, here is the agenda.
4 Would it be possible _____ you to do it?
5 The week _____ March 5 is good for me.

4 將句裏的詞語排成正確順序。

1 OK / me / if / that / date / is / Let / know

_____.

2 ending / is / good / for / me / The / 25 / June / week

_____.

3 this / our / afternoon / here / are / my / Following / notes / meeting

_____.

4 your / for / phone / this / call / morning / Thanks

_____.

5 it / be / for / a / Would / room / you / to / possible / reserve / meeting

_____?

5 閱讀約翰的助理皮雅·萊文發來的電郵，從每題找出錯處並且更正它。

Dear Mr Park

1 following your call yesterday with Mr Carter I have checked his schedule and

2 the week starting Febuary 14th is a good time for him to fly to Seoul.

3 Would it bee possible for you to collect Mr Carter from the airport to take him

4 to your offices? He will arrives on QA 673 from Sydney at 10.00 and will stay until February 20th.

5 As regard the agenda, Mr Carter asks if you will send him a list of the topics

6 you want to discuss. Please late me know if that is OK for you.

7 best regards
Pia Levene, Personal Assistant

Language spotlight

第一類條件句

If you are happy with that, I'll arrive… .
If you want, I'll invite… .

條件句有兩個部份：條件從句和結果從句。我們用第一類條件句表示某些可能在未來發生的事：

If you send the report（條件），I'll give it to my manager（結果）．

翻到 169 頁了解更多資料和做練習。

Writing

6 昨天你收到顧問凱文・梅戚有趣的一封電郵。你要回信提議一個時間讓他可以來你的辦公室拜訪，用這些筆記幫助你。

- Thank him for his email.
- Say his services sound interesting.
- Ask if he can come to visit your office on 12th June in the morning to discuss working together.
- Say your assistant can reserve a hotel if he wants.
- Ask him to let you know if this is possible.

7 現在寫一封電郵回覆這封電郵，用這些筆記幫助自己。

Say 12th June is good for you.
Reserving a hotel room is not necessary.
Ask about the time of the meeting.

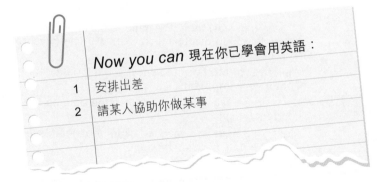

Now you can 現在你已學會用英語：

1 安排出差
2 請某人協助你做某事

14 Priorities for the business trip
出差行程的先後緩急

參與電話會議 | 按先後緩急排序

Telephone conference call

40 CD

1 湯姆、黛安、約翰和凱倫一起開電話會議。聆聽 Track 40 的對話。誰是第一個進入電話會議的人？

Recorded voice	A new participant is entering the call.
Tom	Tom Field here.
Karen	Hi, Tom. I'm here already. John is coming in a minute. How are you?
Tom	Oh, fine. How about you, Karen?
Karen	Great, thanks. I'm looking forward to … .
Recorded voice	Two new participants are entering the call.
John	Hi Karen, hello Tom and Diane. John here.
Diane	And Diane as well. Hello everybody.
Tom	OK, we can start then. We need to make an agenda of topics for me to discuss next week with the guys from APU in Sydney.
Karen	Well, **first of all**, I want to show you the data centre. **That's very important.**
Tom	Yes. I agree. It's much bigger than the data centre in London, I think.
John	Right. And **next** you have to talk to Veronica Mayer. She's the data security manager.
Tom	OK.
Karen	**After that,** you must meet my team here. They can tell you about the developments we plan for our computer systems over the next five years. It's very exciting.

Tom	I'm sure. Then I can see what we have to do about our systems in London.
Karen	**Finally**, we have to decide when Lowis can change their accounting systems to the APU system. We can't wait too long. **That's crucial.**
Diane	Well, it looks like you're going to be busy, Tom!

Business tip

你探訪在另一個國家的同事時，出發前最好先和對方定好活動或行程，這樣才可以確保想見的所有人都見得到。

Understanding

40
CD

2 再聽一次，完成湯姆拜訪 APU 公司的議程。

1 Visit to APU to see _____ .

2 Talk to Veronica Mayer the _____ manager.

3 Meet Karen's team to learn about new _____ for their computer systems.

4 Discuss timing of change to APU _____ systems.

Key phrases

Prioritizing

First of all ... / First .... / Firstly	*Third / Thirdly ... .*
Next	*Finally ... .*
Second / Secondly	*That's very important / crucial.*
After that, ...	

Practice

3 配對以下兩部份，以完成咖啡機的使用說明。

1	First of all,	A	put the money in the slot.
2	Second,	B	put your cup in the machine.
3	After that,	C	you can drink your perfect cup of coffee!
4	Finally,	D	choose the kind of coffee you want and press the button.

4 完成句子。

1 After _____, you need to change your supplier.

2 Finally, we have _____ organize a workshop.

3 There are two problems: first, the product is too expensive and _____ the quality is bad.

4 These are my plans: first _____ all, I'm going to send the report and ...

5 That's very _____, crucial in fact.

5 一位同事問你,有甚麼秘訣可將一天的工作安排得更有成效,請幫他出點主意。

1 First of all, you need to _____ .

2 Next, you should _____ .

3 Third, you can _____ .

4 And finally you can _____ .

Language spotlight

Can 表示 "能力" 或 "可能性"

We <u>can</u> start.

We <u>can't</u> wait.

我們用 can 表示 "一般能力" 或 "現在和未來可能發生的事"。

翻到 170 頁了解更多資料和做練習。

Speaking

6 有時要聽清楚 can 和 can't 的分別很困難,聆聽 Track 41 的句子,並跟着朗讀一次。

41
CD

1 I can phone her.

2 I can't hear you.

3 They can't come today.

4 He can speak Japanese.

5 We can't pay them.

6 They can start work tomorrow.

7 When can you start?

8 Why can't you do it today?

7 你正在和同事渡邊純在電話對話，他希望來你的公司探訪。在播放錄音之前閱讀提示和回應。播放 Track 42，然後在嗶一聲後説話，再聆聽 Track 43 比較你的對話。

42–43
CD

Jun So I'm coming to visit you and other people next month. What topics should we discuss?

You *(1 / can / discuss / project schedule)*

Jun Good idea. What next?

You *(2 / have to check / project costs)*

Jun I agree. And after that?

You *(After / must talk about / problems with / consultants)*

Jun Yes, that is a big problem. Anything else?

You *(Finally / have to / go out for dinner)*

Jun That's a very good idea!

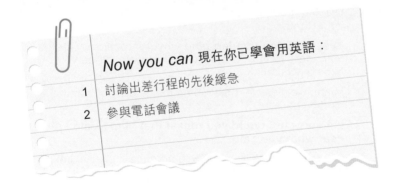

Now you can 現在你已學會用英語：

1　討論出差行程的先後緩急

2　參與電話會議

15 Dealing with questions in the conference call
處理電話會議的提問

請求重複 | 請求解釋 | 提出建議

Telephone conference call

44 CD

1 湯姆、黛安、約翰和凱倫仍然在開電話會議，聆聽 Track 44 的對話。黛安建議了甚麼，約翰又對她的建議有甚麼看法？

Diane	Well, we've agreed on Tom's agenda. But John, I think we should organize a conference for the senior management level of Lowis and APU. I think it could really help us all.
John	Hmm. **Is there a reason why** you think it's important at the moment?
Diane	Well, I think it would be a good idea for the managers to get together so that we can all see why changes at Lowis are so important.
John	**Yes, but I don't understand why** it's necessary for the managers from APU to take part as well. It'll be very expensive then.
Diane	Mmm, well it's clear that some things are not working as well as they could.
John	**I'm sorry but could you repeat that? I'm afraid I didn't hear what you said**.
Diane	Oh, sorry. I think if the people here meet the APU managers, everybody will be able to work together better.
Tom	And we can deal with some misunderstandings.
Karen	**What do you mean by** 'misunderstandings'?
Tom	Well, we think we ought to improve the communication.
John	I see. **Can you give an example?**

Diane	Well, for some managers at Lowis it's difficult to understand why the changes are necessary. To the accounting systems, for example. We shouldn't wait until people here begin to cause problems.
John	Hmm. Yes, in that case maybe that is a good idea, Diane. I think you and I should send an invitation to the key people. When do you think would be a good date and where should we have the conference?

Business tip

你不清楚生意伙伴用英語講甚麼時，你應該請他們重新解釋，這樣可以避免誤會，並留心發問時語氣要有禮貌。

Understanding

2 再聽一次，選擇最合適的答案。

44
CD

1 Diane wants to organize a conference for

   A the old managers.

   B the managers with high positions in the company.

   C the young managers.

2 Diane wants to organize a conference so that

   A the APU managers understand what they have to do.

   B the Lowis managers understand what they have to do.

   C the APU and the Lowis managers understand what they have to do.

3 John wants

   A Karen to send the invitations.

   B Tom to send the invitations.

   C Diane and himself to send the invitations.

Key phrases

1 Asking for repetition

I'm sorry but could you repeat that?	I'm afraid / sorry I didn't hear what you said.

2 Asking for explanations

Is there a reason why ...?	What do you mean by ... ?
Yes, but I don't understand why	Can you give an example?

3 配對以下兩部份。

1 What do you mean by 'difficult'?

2 Can you give an example?

3 Could you repeat that?

4 Is there a reason why you're late?

A Sure. Last week I called your hotline and …

B I said the 21st April.

C Well, my train was late.

D I mean it's not easy.

4 將句裏的詞語排成正確順序。

1 word / sorry / could / I'm / repeat / you / that / last / but

_____?

2 do / mean / you / by / 'delayed' / What

_____?

3 I / a / understand / But / why / it's / don't / problem

_____.

4 you / this / give / example / me / an / Can / of

_____?

5 完成句子。

1 **A:** _____ understand. Why _____ difficult?

B: It's difficult because we don't have the money.

2 **A:** Can _____ example?

B: Yes, of course. The software doesn't work.

3 **A:** Is _____ you haven't paid us?

B: Yes. We don't have any money at the moment.

4 **A:** _____ sorry. _____ that?

B: Yes, I said 'delayed'.

5 **A:** _____ understand _____ her job is.

B: Data security. She's the data security manager.

Language spotlight

should / shouldn't / ought to 表示強烈推薦

We <u>should</u> organize a conference.

We <u>ought to</u> improve communication.

We <u>shouldn't</u> wait.

should 和 *ought to* 同樣表示應做某事。*shouldn't* 用於表示不應做某事。

翻到 171 頁了解更多資料和做練習。

Speaking

6 當你請求解釋時，聽起來禮貌很重要，聆聽 Track 45 的句子，並跟着朗讀一次。

45
CD

1 Is there a reason why we can't do it this month?
2 Yes, but I don't understand why we have to wait.
3 What do you mean by a small delay?
4 Can you give an example?

7 你正和公司的供應商在電話裏討論一個問題。在播放錄音之前閱讀提示和回應。播放 Track 46，然後在嗶一聲後説話，再聆聽 Track 47 比較你的對話。

46–47
CD

Supplier	Then there was a strike at the factory.
You	*(Ask him to repeat that.)*
Supplier	There was a strike.
You	*(Say you don't understand the word.)*
Supplier	Oh, I see. A strike. It means the workers stopped working.
You	*(Say you understand now. Ask why they had a strike now.)*
Supplier	Well, they weren't happy with the new terms and conditions.
You	*(Ask for an example.)*
Supplier	Well, first the workers wanted more money.
You	*(Ask for repetition. You didn't hear the last word.)*
Supplier	The workers wanted more money.

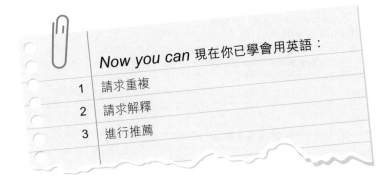

Now you can 現在你已學會用英語：

1 請求重複
2 請求解釋
3 進行推薦

16 Written invitations 撰寫邀請

撰寫商業邀請 | 回覆商業邀請

Email

1 黛安和約翰同意為洛維工程公司和 APU 公司的高層管理人員舉辦一次會議。閱讀電郵邀請和回覆。會議在甚麼地方和時間舉行？維·桑達會不會出席？

Subject: **Save the date**

Dear **Colleagues**

We are pleased to invite you to the first joint senior management conference for Australian Power Utilities and Lowis Engineering. **The event will take place on** January 10 in London.

This occasion will be an opportunity to meet your new colleagues and network with them. **We would be grateful if you could** email us if you can attend by Wednesday November 4.

As soon as we receive your answer, we will send more information including a detailed agenda, list of speakers, planned activities and hotel reservation forms.

We look forward to welcoming you to London **in the near future**.

Yours truly

Diane Kennedy & John Carter

Dear Diane and John

Thanks very much for your invitation to the conference. I think this is a very good idea.

I planned to go to our Brazil office during that week but will try to change this.

When I know I can change this trip, I will get back to you to confirm my attendance.

Best wishes
Ray Saunders

Business tip

寫一封重要電郵給其他同事時，要肯定你用一些字眼吸引他們的注意力，例如用 Save the date 作為電郵主旨。

Understanding

2 再看一次電郵，判斷以下句子是正確 T 還是錯誤 F？

1 The email is sent to customers of APU and Lowis.   T / F
2 Participants will have a chance to get to know each other.   T / F
3 Diane and John want people to telephone them with their answer. T / F
4 The information about the conference is all on the email.   T / F
5 Participants will stay at a hotel.   T / F
6 Ray Saunders can definitely attend the conference.   T / F

Key phrases

A formal email invitation

Save the date	*We would be grateful if you … .*
Dear Colleagues	*We look forward to welcoming you*
We are pleased to invite you to … .	*to … in the near future*
The event will take place on … .	*Yours truly*
This occasion will be an opportunity to network with … .	

Practice

3 找出每題遺漏的字詞，填在橫線上。

1 We are pleased invite you to the opening of our new offices in Penang.
_____

2 We would be grateful you inform us about your plans. _____

3 We forward to welcoming you to our new offices in the near future.
_____

4 This occasion be an opportunity to meet senior managers. _____

4 找出每題的錯處並且更正它。

1 Please save the dade. _____

2 The conference will take plaice on April 23. _____

3 We look forward to seeing you in the next future. _____

4 Yours Truly _____

5 This conference will be an opportunity too meet the staff.
_____

5 你同事寫了一封邀請函，邀請顧客出席展示最新產品的銷售會議，她想你幫她檢查一下。以下已標示的部份過於非正式，請改寫它們，令其更恰當、更正式。

Dear Mr Hunter

1) We want you to come to our sales conference on September 13.
Please save the date.

2) It's going to be in the Tower Hotel.

3) It'll be a great chance for you to meet our staff.
We look forward to welcoming you to London in the near future.

4) Cheers,

---

1 _____

2 _____

3 _____

4 _____

Language spotlight

時間短語

我們可以用 as soon as / when / after / before 等詞語或短語連接句子。

As soon as we receive your answer, we will send an... .

When I know I can change this trip, I will get back to you to... .

翻到 171 頁了解更多資料和做練習。

Writing

6 你的上司占士·史葛想你替他邀請公司高層的管理人員出席德國慕尼黑新工廠的開幕典禮。用以下的筆記撰寫邀請信。

> Factory opening – April 4 (10:00 am)
>
> Opportunity to see new equipment
> in action
>
> Reply before March 1
>
> As soon as reply received – details of
> event, location and hotel
>
> Look forward to meet at factory
> opening

7 撰寫邀請信的回覆，説你不確定你能否出席，但會盡快回覆占士。

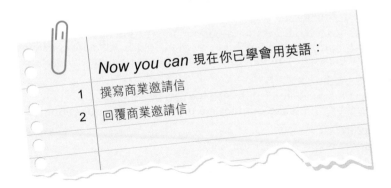

Now you can 現在你已學會用英語：

| 1 | 撰寫商業邀請信 |
| 2 | 回覆商業邀請信 |

提供酒店資料 | 談及現時的活動

Email

1 約翰・卡特的行政助理皮雅・萊文發了一封電郵給湯姆。為甚麼她寫電郵給湯姆？

Dear Mr Field

Let me introduce myself – I am Mr Carter's administrative assistant and **I would like to confirm** your hotel arrangements.

I have booked you into the Southern Cross Hotel for seven nights (October 17-24). The hotel has sent me a confirmation code for your reservation, TF18OCT24210.

The hotel has a limousine service and, if you send me your flight details, **I will arrange for** you to be picked up from the airport. **For detailed information about** the hotel facilities, **please check their website**:

www.southern-cross.aus

Mr Carter has reserved tickets for a performance of the opera *Carmen* at the Sydney Opera House on the Saturday evening. He will meet you in the hotel lobby at 6.30 pm. **You can find** reviews of the production here:

www.sydney_echo.com

I look forward to welcoming you to Sydney and the offices of APU on Monday October 20. **Please contact me if you have any questions.**

Yours sincerely

Pia Levene

Business tip

如果為重要的外國訪客安排出差，要找出他們喜歡的東西，如音樂、運動、戲劇、博物館和餐廳等，以便為他們安排到訪後的社交活動。

Understanding

2 再讀一次電郵，回答以下問題。

1 Who will pick Tom up from the airport?
2 What does Pia want Tom to send her?
3 Where can Tom find out if the hotel has a swimming pool?
4 Where will John take Tom on Saturday?

Key phrases

Looking after visitors

Let me introduce myself – I'm	*Please check ... .*
I would like to confirm	*You can find ... .*
I will arrange for	*Please contact me if you have any questions.*
For detailed information about	

Practice

3 配對以下兩部份，組成完整句子。

1 I would like to confirm
2 Please check your
3 You can
4 I will arrange
5 For detailed

A find information ... .
B your reservation.
C for your taxi to arrive at ... .
D information, please ... .
E credit card details.

4 將句裏的詞語排成正確順序。

1 will / photocopied / documents / arrange / for / the / Jasmine / be / to

_____ .

2 I / to / Singapore Airport / like / would / your / landing / confirm / time / at.

_____ .

3 find / document / more / details / in / the / can / attached / You

_____ .

4 introduce / me / Let / myself / – / name's / Goodman / my / Jasmine

_____ .

5 call / any / you / me / if / have / Please / problems

_____ .

5 閱讀黛安的助理茉莉・歌文的電郵，從每題找出錯處並且更正它。

Dear Ms Taylor

(1) Let my introduce myself – I am Diane Kennedy's assistant and I am writing to you

(2) because I will like to confirm details about your visit next week.

(3) I have reserved meeting room 715 for you and I will arrange four coffee

(4) and water. A multimedia projector are available in the room for presentations.

(5) I have booked you into the Tower Hotel from October 12-15. For detail information,

(6) please cheque the hotel's website (**www.towerhotel.co.uk**).

(7) Please contact me if you has any questions.

Yours sincerely

Jasmine Goodman

(1) _____ (2) _____ (3) _____ (4) _____ (5) _____
(6) _____ (7) _____

Language spotlight

現在完成式

I **have booked** you into the Southern Cross Hotel for seven nights.
The hotel **has sent** me a confirmation code for your reservation.
Mr Carter **has reserved** tickets for a performance of the opera Carmen.
我們用現在完成式談論近期活動。

翻到 172 頁了解更多資料和練習。

Writing

6 上司請你寫電郵給一個新客戶，凱特・本德。凱特要到你的公司參加一個會議，然後和你上司一起吃晚飯。用以下資料寫電郵給本德女士。

- Introduce yourself.
- Hotel details: Harunami Hotel, three nights (March 23-26).
- Confirmation code: HH23MAR211
- Further information www.harunami_hotel.com
- Restaurant table reserved March 24. Boss will meet hotel lobby 7.00 pm
- Contact you with any questions.

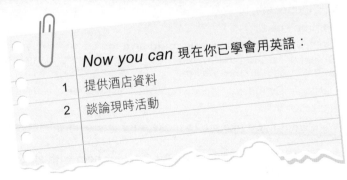

Now you can 現在你已學會用英語：

| 1 | 提供酒店資料 |
| 2 | 談論現時活動 |

18 Changes to the schedule 更改日程

提供協助 ｜ 提出請求 ｜ 道謝

1 聆聽 Track 48，湯姆·菲特和悉尼的皮雅·萊文正在通電話。現在湯姆會留在澳洲多少天？

Pia	Pia Levene, **how can I help you?**
Tom	Oh hello, Pia. This is Tom Field from Lowis Engineering in London.
Pia	Oh hello, Tom. **What can I do for you?**
Tom	Well, first of all, **thanks very much for** arranging my hotel for me.
Pia	My pleasure.
Tom	**I wonder if I could ask you for a favour**. **Could I make a small change** to the schedule?
Pia	Of course.
Tom	**Please could you change** my hotel reservation so that I arrive on October the 16th?
Pia	No problem.
Tom	And **I wanted to ask if you could arrange** for me to have a rental car for the Sunday, the 19th. I have some friends to visit up the coast. Just a small car.
Pia	Certainly. By the way, have you visited Sydney before, Tom?
Tom	No, I haven't.
Pia	Well, **would you like me to make sure** the rental company gives you a satnav in the car? So you don't get lost.
Tom	That's a great idea. **Thanks a lot for your help with all the arrangements,** Pia.

Pia	No worries.
Tom	And **would you mind sending me an email** with the details again? **That would be really kind.**
Pia	Of course not.

Understanding

48
CD

2 再聽一次對話，皮雅在和湯姆對話的時候寫了一些筆記，她的筆記有甚麼錯處？

1 Tom Field – Lowis Engineering
2 Wants to change hotel
3 Arrive Sydney Oct 16
4 Rental car 18-19 Oct
5 Visited Sydney already
6 Send letter confirming details

Key phrases

1 Offering help

How can I help you?	Would you like me to ...?
What can I do for you?	

2 Making a request

I wonder if I can ask you for a favour?	I wanted to ask if you could ... .
Please could I / you change ...?	Would you mind sending me an email?

3 Giving thanks

Thanks very much for ...+ing	That would be really kind.
Thanks a lot for your help with the arrangements.	

Practice

3 配對以下兩部份，組成完整句子。

1 Would you like me to make reservations?

2 I wonder if I can ask you for a favour?

3 Thanks a lot for your help.

4 Please could you change the meeting room?

5 Would you mind saying that again?

A Of course. Which one would you like?

B My pleasure.

C Sure. What would you like me to do for you?

D For dinner? That would be really kind!

E Of course not.

4 完成句子。

1 How _____ we help you?

2 I wanted to _____ if you could send me the files ...

3 _____ you like me to make sure they're sent by courier?

4 That would be really _____.

5 Thanks a _____ for your help with the project.

5 黛安的助理茉莉收到伊娃·舒默茲的電話，談及下星期伊娃到訪洛維工程公司的安排。將句子排成正確順序，完成對話，然後聆聽 Track 49 核對答案。

1	Jasmine	Jasmine Goodman, Lowis Engineering London. How can I help you?
	Eva	No, it's OK thank you. I'll take the underground. But thanks a lot for your help with the arrangements.
	Jasmine	Fine. Would you like me to organize for you to be met at the airport when you arrive?
	Eva	That's right.
	Jasmine	My pleasure!
	Eva	Well, you booked me a room at the Tower Hotel for three nights. Would you mind changing the reservation to only one night? For the last two nights I'm going to stay with friends.
	Jasmine	Of course, Ms Schmidt. What can I do for you?
	Eva	Hello. This is Eva Schmidt here. I wonder if I could ask you a favour.
	Jasmine	No problem. So you only want a room for October 31st?

Language spotlight

一般現在完成式 － 否定和疑問

Have you visited Sydney before?

Yes, I have. / No, I haven't.

我們會用現在完成式提問和回答問題，這些問題關於沒有實際時間的過去經驗。

翻到 172 頁了解更多資料和做練習。

Speaking

50
CD

6　當你請人幫你做事和回應時，聽起來有禮貌是很重要的。聆聽 Track 50，然後跟着朗讀這些請求和回應。

　1　**A:** I wonder if I can ask you for a favour?
　　　B: Of course. How can I help?

　2　**A:** Please could I change my reservation?
　　　B: No problem. I'll do that now.

　3　**A:** I wanted to ask if you could send me a brochure.
　　　B: No worries. I'll do that today.

　4　**A:** Would you mind sending me an email?
　　　B: Of course not.

51–52
CD

7　你打電話給重要生意伙伴何先生的助理法蘭，你想更改下星期到訪何先生公司的日程。在播放錄音前閱讀提示和回應，然後播放 Track 51，在嗶一聲後説話。再聆聽 Track 52 比較你的對話。

Frank　Frank Richards speaking.
You　*(Say your name and ask if he can help you).*
Frank　Of course. What can I do for you?
You　*(Ask if you can change your meeting time with Mr Ho.)*
Frank　I'm sure we can find a time. When is convenient?
You　*(Ask if ten o'clock on Tuesday would be possible.)*
Frank　Let me see … well, I need to change another appointment of Mr Ho's, but that's not a problem.
You　*(Great! Thank Frank for all his help with the arrangements.)*
Frank　My pleasure!

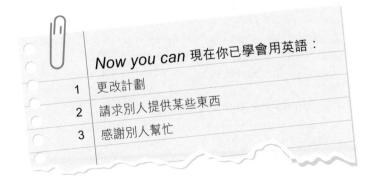

Now you can 現在你已學會用英語：

1　更改計劃
2　請求別人提供某些東西
3　感謝別人幫忙

19 Welcome back to the office 歡迎回到公司

閒談 | 談及出差 | 查詢進度

Video

07
DVD

1 在湯姆去完澳洲出差之後，他看見他的經理黛安，閱讀對話並觀看短片。為甚麼湯姆不喜歡他飛行的航班？

Diane	Ah, Tom! **Good to see you again!**
Tom	Hello, Diane. **It's good to be back.**
Diane	**Good flight?**
Tom	Oh, **it was awful**! We had to land in a very cold Moscow because of a technical problem. We stayed there for six hours.
Diane	Oh, dear. **Well, it's nice to have you back. Is everything going well,** do you think, with APU? Did you get my email on Friday?
Tom	About the APU-Lowis joint management conference? Yes. I think the APU people are really interested in the idea. I can give you more details in the project meeting later.
Diane	Great. So, **what did you get up to** in Sydney? I remember they have some very good Italian restaurants.
Tom	Yeah! But the best restaurants were the Japanese sushi bars.
Diane	**Did you do any sightseeing?**
Tom	Yes, a little. John and his wife took me to Sydney Opera House to see *Carmen*.
Diane	**Lucky you!**

Tom	Yeah, it was a nice evening. My hotel room was overlooking Sydney harbour. It's the most amazing place.
Diane	**What was the weather like?**
Tom	**Great**! Lots of sunshine and really hot. On the hottest day I think it was about thirty-five degrees. It rained here, didn't it?
Diane	Yes, every day last week!

Business tip

同事出差或度假回公司上班時，可以與他們閒談旅程的所見所聞，這是有禮貌的表現。如果你沒有這樣做，他們可能覺得你不關心他們。

Understanding

07
DVD

2 再看一次短片，為每題選取最合適的答案。

1 In Sydney, Tom
   A had a vacation.
   B worked all the time.
   C did some sightseeing.

3 Last week the weather was best in
   A Sydney.
   B London.
   C Moscow.

2 Tom thinks the APU managers
   A like the idea of a joint conference.
   B don't like the idea of a joint conference.
   C are planning a joint conference.

Key phrases

1 Making small talk	
Good to see you again.	*Well, it's good / nice to have you back.*
It's good / nice to be back.	
2 Asking about and describing past experiences	
Good flight?	*Lucky you!*
What did you get up to / do?	*It was awful!*
Did you do any sightseeing?	*Great!*
What was the weather like?	
3 Checking progress	
Is everything going well with ... ?	*Is everything OK with ... ?*

3 參考 Key phrases 完成句子。

1 _____ to be back!   4 _____ you again!

2 _____ the weather like?   5 _____ get up to?

3 _____ any sightseeing?   6 _____ have you back!

4 將句裏的詞語排成正確順序。

1 did / get / Paris / up / you / to / What / in

_____ ?

2 the / like / weather / What / when / you / Seattle / were / was / in

_____ ?

3 she / there / do / any / Did / sightseeing / she / when / was

_____ ?

4 everything / in / going / Shanghai / Is / well

_____ ?

5 to / again / see / Good / you

_____ !

5 閱讀羅拔和茉莉的對話，將句子排成正確順序後聆聽 Track 53。

53
CD

	Robert	Some. I saw the Great Wall.
1	Robert	Hi Jasmine. Good to see you again!
	Robert	No, it was awful. But Bejing was great!
	Jasmine	Really? Did you do any sightseeing?
	Robert	Yes, Diane told me. But still, it's nice to be back!
	Jasmine	Fantastic! What was the weather like?
	Robert	Oh, great. On the hottest day it was about 35 degrees!
	Jasmine	Lucky you. It rained here.
	Jasmine	Hello, Robert. Nice to have you back! Good flight?

Language spotlight

形容詞最高級形式

But the best restaurants... .   *It's the most amazing place.*
On the hottest day... .

最高級形式是這樣構成的：短詞語如 hot，加 -est 變成 hottest。長詞語如 amazing，加 most 變成 the most amazing。

翻到 168 頁了解更多資料和做練習。

Speaking

6 當你用 did you 提問時，這兩個字會連讀。聆聽 Track 54，然後跟着朗讀句子。

54 CD

1 What <u>did you</u> say?

2 <u>Did you</u> go sightseeing?

3 <u>Did you</u> have a good flight?

4 When <u>did you</u> fly back?

5 How <u>did you</u> know?

6 What <u>did you</u> buy?

7 你的朋友凱絲剛從紐約出差回來，和她說話。在播放錄音前閱讀提示和回應，然後播放 Track 55，在呸一聲後說話。再聆聽 Track 56 比較你的對話。

55–56 CD

Cathy	Hello! Good to see you again.
You	*(Say it's nice to have her back again and ask if she had a good flight.)*
Cathy	Yes, it was fine.
You	*(Ask if everything is OK in the New York office.)*
Cathy	Yes. I had a very interesting time.
You	*(Ask if she went sightseeing.)*
Cathy	No, not really. But I did go shopping!
You	*(Lucky her! Ask her what she bought.)*
Cathy	Well, I went to Bloomingdale's because I've always wanted to go there. I bought a bag.
You	*(Ask about the weather there.)*
Cathy	Oh, it was good. Sunny and warm.
You	*(Say it was very cold here.)*
Cathy	Oh, dear.

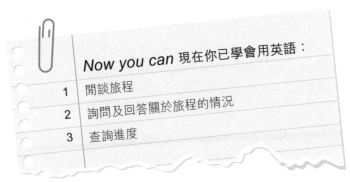

Now you can 現在你已學會用英語：

1 閒談旅程

2 詢問及回答關於旅程的情況

3 查詢進度

20　The project review 檢討項目

檢討項目 ｜ 詢問進度 ｜ 提供解釋

Video

08
DVD

1 湯姆要告訴經理黛安有關資訊科技系統的整合狀態，閱讀對話並觀看短片。有甚麼工作進度落後了？

Diane	So, Tom, are you saying that John and Karen aren't happy about the project's progress?
Tom	Yes. They say we're too slow.
Diane	**Let's look at** the project plan then.
Tom	OK. So, **here we can see** all the main IT topics: integration of the human resources systems, the integration of accounting and bookkeeping and the integration of sales data.
Diane	**Can you show me** the project status?
Tom	**Well, the next diagram shows** the detailed schedule for all the HR systems: payroll, social security, performance review, training records. All integrated into the APU systems.
Diane	Great! Have you started the training programme for the HR people on the new system yet?
Tom	Oh, we've finished that already. We did that last month.
Diane	Good. So **when will you finish** everything else?
Tom	Well, **moving on to** the integration of our accounting systems, I'm afraid that's late. We haven't transferred all the data to APU yet.
Diane	Oh. **Can you explain why not?**
Tom	APU collects its information in a different way to us. That's one problem.

Diane	But **I don't understand why** that's a problem. It's the same information in different boxes.
Tom	The biggest problem is that Robert's accounting team is too small to do all the work. But I've told them they have to finish by the end of January.
Diane	Really? **When did you do that?**
Tom	I had a telephone conference call with them last week when I was in Sydney.
Diane	I see. That's good.
Tom	Moving on?
Diane	Sure.

Business tip

不必害怕檢討項目之後別人發問，因這是個好現象，發問表示別人對你講的內容感興趣，也給你機會再講解別人最感興趣的內容要點。

Understanding

08
DVD

2 再看一次短片，以下句子是正確 (T) 還是錯誤 (F)？

1 John and Karen are happy with the project. T / F
2 Tom has to bring the computer systems from Lowis and APU together. T / F
3 The training for the HR systems is finished. T / F
4 The accounting systems are already integrated. T / F
5 Robert doesn't have enough people. T / F

Key phrases

1 Using slides in a project review	2 Asking questions at a project review
Let's look at … .	Can you show me …?
Here we can see … .	Have you … yet?
The next slide / diagram shows … .	When will you finish …?
Moving on to … .	Can you explain why …?
	I don't understand why … .
	When did you (do) that?

3 配對以下兩部份，組成完整句子。

1 Have you finished
2 Let's look at
3 I don't understand why
4 Moving on to
5 When will you finish

A it's the most expensive company.
B the second slide, we can see the problem.
C the figures.
D the first part of the project?
E the report yet?

4 公司同事正匯報一個工作項目，用你自己的資料，就有關項目提問題，並且完成句子。

1 Can you show me _____ ?
2 I don't understand why _____ ?
3 When did you _____ ?
4 Have you written _____ yet?
5 When will you _____ ?

5 湯姆為同事做一個項目匯報，按投影片的主題完成句子。

1 Schedule   _____ the project schedule.
2 Costs   _____ problems with the costs.
3 Quality   _____ question of quality, … .
4 Next steps   _____ next steps.

Language spotlight

Already 和 yet

Have you started the training programme yet?
Oh, we've finished that already.
I'm afraid we haven't transferred all the data to APU yet.

我們用 yet 和 already 配合現在完成式，來詢問和回答有關現時活動的問題。

翻到 173 頁了解更多資料和做練習。

Speaking

6 讓伙伴知道一句句子裏某項資料很重要的簡單方法，是將某個詞語用重音讀出。重音能改變句子含義，聆聽 Track 57 的句子。

Have YOU finished the report? (YOU, nobody else)
Have you FINISHED the report? (Is the report completed?)
Have you finished the REPORT? (The REPORT, not the email)

聆聽及朗讀以下句子，重讀粗體字詞。

1 Have you **seen** Tom this afternoon yet? [meaning not spoken to him]
2 Have you seen **Tom** this afternoon yet? [meaning not Diane]
3 Have you seen Tom this **afternoon** yet? [meaning not this morning]
4 Have **you** seen Tom this afternoon yet? [meaning not someone else]

7 你是經理，而你的團隊組員正在匯報有關她項目的資料，問她一些問題。在播放錄音前閱讀提示和回應，然後播放 Track 58，在呲一聲後説話。再聆聽 Track 59 比較你的對話。

Team member	So let's look at the project status then. Here we can see the costs so far.
You	*(Ask if she can show you the time schedule.)*
Team member	Yes, well the next slide shows the detailed schedule for the system integration and the training programme.
You	*(Ask if she has started the training programme yet.)*
Team member	No, we haven't started it yet.
You	*(Say you don't understand why not.)*
Team member	Well, the equipment isn't ready yet.
You	*(Ask when it will be ready.)*
Team member	It'll be ready by the end of this week. But we've finished the software update already.
You	*(Good! Ask when they did that.)*
Team member	That was on Friday last week.

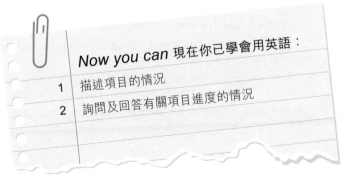

Now you can 現在你已學會用英語：

1 描述項目的情況
2 詢問及回答有關項目進度的情況

21 Starting the video conference
開始視像會議

參與視像會議 | 描述技術問題 | 處理延誤

09
DVD

1 在倫敦的湯姆和黛安與在悉尼的約翰和凱倫開始視像會議。閱讀對話，和觀看短片。他們可以解決技術問題嗎？

Diane	So I just put in the numbers … like that … and then we should be able to see John and Karen.
	And there they are. This video conferencing equipment is fantastic! Hi John, hi Karen, can you hear us? **Sorry, your sound doesn't seem to be working!**
Karen	… and if we press this button, we should be able to hear them. Ah! There's Diane! Can you hear us?
Diane	That's much better.
Karen	**Just a moment.** Now **there seems to be something wrong with the picture.**
Karen	Diane, Tom? **I'm having trouble with the picture.** Can you see us?
Tom	Yes, and we can hear you too!
John	Well, **I think our system has crashed!** We can't see anything!
Karen	Oh, I don't understand. **When I click on the start button, nothing happens.**
John	**Sorry to keep you waiting, Diane.** Karen can't work this thing and I don't know what to do either.
Karen	**I think I need to call a technician. Hold on a minute!**
Diane	Don't worry. I completely understand. We can wait.

Business tip

如果你在匯報、開會或見面時需要使用電子器材，請確定：
1 使用器材之前半小時，你檢查過它們可以操作。
2 器材若出現問題，你打電話可找到人解決問題。

Understanding

09
DVD

2 再看一次短片，回答以下問題。

1 Who has a problem with their technical equipment, Diane and Tom or Karen and John?
2 What is their problem?
3 What do they do about their problem?

Key phrases

1 Describing technical problems	2 Dealing with delays
There seems to be something wrong with … .	*Just a moment.*
I'm having trouble with … .	*Hold on a minute.*
I think my XYZ has crashed.	*Sorry to keep you waiting.*
The XYZ doesn't seem to be working.	
When I click on the XYZ, nothing happens.	
I think I need to call a technician.	

Practice

3 從方框找出合適字詞完成句子。

click keep on trouble wrong

1 Sorry to _____ you waiting.
2 When I _____ on the Word icon, nothing happens!
3 There seems to be something _____ with the remote control.
4 Hold _____ a minute, please.
5 I'm having _____ with my cell phone.

4 將句裏的詞語排成正確順序。

1 We're / server / having / with / trouble / the

　　　_____ .

2 need / think / to / I / call / the / we / help / desk

　　　_____ .

3 a / Just / please / moment,

　　　_____ .

4 I / email / my / open / account, / When / computer / crashes / my

　　　_____ .

5 telephone / to / seem / The / doesn't / working / be

　　　_____ .

5 遇到以下情況時，你會對電腦服務熱線説甚麼：

1 Your computer has a blue screen?
  My system _____ .

2 The computer is working but you can't open your email account?
  I'm having _____ .

3 You can't print a document?
  There seems _____ .

4 Your internet connection isn't working?
  The internet doesn't _____ .

5 You have to check your computer details before you can answer a question?
  Sorry _____ .

Language spotlight

Too 和 not...either

Yes, and we can hear you <u>too</u>!

Karen can't work this thing and I don't know what to do <u>either</u>.

Too 與 as well 和 also 都有同樣意思。這些字詞通常置於句尾。若想用否定式，我們會用 not...either。

翻到 173 頁了解更多資料和做練習。

Speaking

6 當有人跟你説他們發生了一些不好的事，你需要回應他們。聆聽 Track 60，然後跟着朗讀句子。

60 CD

1 Oh no!
2 Sorry to hear that!
3 That's terrible!
4 I am sorry!
5 That's awful!

7 你的電腦有些問題，你打電話去服務熱線找人幫忙。在播放錄音前閲讀提示和回應，然後播放 Track 61，在呸一聲後説話。再聆聽 Track 62 比較你的對話。

61–62 CD

Help desk	How can I help you?
You	*(Tell her there is something wrong with your computer.)*
Help desk	OK. What's the matter?
You	*(Say you're having trouble with the screen.)*
Help desk	OK. Have you tried to reboot your computer?
You	*(Say when you click on the restart icon nothing happens.)*
Help desk	Have you tried to turn off the computer and then restart?
You	*(Ask her to wait a moment.)*
Help desk	No problem.
You	*(Say you are sorry to keep her waiting. Then say you need a technician.)*
Help desk	OK, I'll come up to your office.
You	*(Say thanks.)*

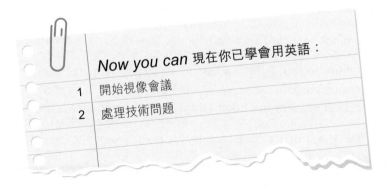

Now you can 現在你已學會用英語：

1　開始視像會議

2　處理技術問題

22　Discussing problems in the video conference 在視像會議上討論問題

在會議中表示同意 | 在會議中表示不同意

Video

10
DVD

1 解決了技術問題之後，湯姆、黛安、約翰和凱倫繼續他們的視像會議，討論洛維和 APU 公司的整合問題。閱讀對話和觀看短片，黛安需要做甚麼？

John	Oh good! We can see and hear you now! Thanks, Tony.
Diane	Excellent! So we need to discuss the progress of the project, I think.
Karen	**That's right**. The integration of the human resources and the sales departments has gone well. It's just your accountants that are a problem. They don't seem to want to use our IT accounting system so they do everything slowly!
Diane	**I don't agree**, Karen. Our accountants have to check your system carefully to be sure …
Karen	**Yes, but** it's three months now! I think you need to put more pressure on Robert Holden's team.
Tom	**I'm not sure that's going to work.** They don't have enough people for all their tasks at the moment. They need help.
Diane	**I think so too.** They need more resources, not more pressure.
John	Maybe I should talk to Robert and explain why it's so important.
Diane	Look, **I'm sorry but I don't think that's a good idea**. Robert knows why it's important. We just have to give him more time.
Karen	**I'm afraid that's not possible.** We have to integrate the systems before the new financial year starts in January.
John	**Yes, I agree**. You can't run a business without financial information.
Diane	**You're absolutely right.** So let's see if we can find another solution to this problem.

Business tip

在商業運作裏，雙方意見分歧很常見，但不同文化表達同意或不同意有不同方法。如果你和不同文化的人開會，記住要先了解在對方的文化裏，是用甚麼方法表示同意或不同意的。

Understanding

10
DVD

2 再看一次短片，以下句子是正確 (T) 還是錯誤 (F) ？

1	The accounting department integration is going well.	T / F
2	Karen thinks the accounting department is working slowly.	T / F
3	Diane agrees with Karen.	T / F
4	The accounting team has enough people.	T / F
5	Diane wants to find a solution to the problem.	T / F

Key phrases

1 Agreeing	2 Disagreeing
That's right.	*I don't agree.*
Yes, I agree.	*Yes, but … .*
I think so too.	*I'm not sure that's going to work.*
You're absolutely right.	*I'm sorry but I don't think that's a good idea.*
	I'm afraid that's not possible.

Practice

3 配對以下兩部份，組成完整句子。

1	She's absolutely	**A**	too.
2	We're not sure	**B**	right.
3	I'm afraid	**C**	agree.
4	They think so	**D**	that's going to work.
5	He doesn't	**E**	that's not possible.

4 公司同事正匯報一個工作項目，用你自己的資料，就有關項目提問題，並且完成句子。

1 Mr Brauer isn't _____ that's going to work.

2 I'm _____ but we don't think that's a good idea.

3 I'm afraid that's _____ possible.

4 They're _____ right.

5 We think _____ too.

5 湯姆為同事做一個項目匯報，按投影片的主題完成句子。

1	Fiona	We need to open a new office in Moscow for our Russian customers. What do you think?
	Simon	Yes, I agree. We need to be close to our customers.
	Fiona	I'm sorry but I don't think that's a good idea, Simon!
	Tom	Yes, but at the moment we don't have any customers there, do we?
	Simon	We need to remember the costs. You're quite right. Perhaps we should close the office in Sydney and then open an office in Moscow.
	Simon	I don't agree. We have some business with Vladivoil. We need to increase that.
	Tom	I'm sorry but I don't think it's a good idea. It's very expensive to open an office in Russia.
	Fiona	I think so too. Russia is the next big market.

Language spotlight

副詞

They do everything so <u>slowly</u>!
Our accountants have to check your system <u>carefully</u>.
The integration... has gone <u>well</u>.

副詞用來描述動詞。規則副詞的構成通常在形容詞之後加 *-ly*，如 *strong* 變成 *strongly*，或結尾若是 *y*，形容詞之後變成 *-ily*，如 *pretty* 變成 *prettily*。形容詞 *good* 是一個例外，副詞會變成 *well*。

翻到 174 頁了解更多資料和做練習。

Speaking

6 當你不同意別人的看法時，聽起來有禮貌是很重要的。聆聽 Track 64，然後跟着朗讀句子。

1 I'm sorry but I don't agree with you.
2 Yes, but that's too late, I'm afraid.
3 I'm not sure that's going to work.
4 I'm sorry but I think that's a bad idea.
5 I'm afraid that just isn't going to be possible.

7 你和美國的同事戴爾開會，討論你們公司的資訊科技策略。在播放錄音前閱讀提示和回應，然後播放 Track 65，在嗶一聲後説話。再聆聽 Track 66 比較你的對話。

65–66
CD

Dale	Well, the next point on the agenda is IT strategy. We need to decide what to do next about our business management system.
You	*(Agree.)*
Dale	In the US we think we need to update our business management system.
You	*(Disagree and say you think the present system is fine.)*
Dale	But the new system is really easy to use!
You	*(Disagree and say you think the new system has problems.)*
Dale	Well, the present system does work well.
You	*(Agree.)*
Dale	But the new system is much faster.
	(Suggest you continue the discussion at lunch.)
Dale	Good idea!

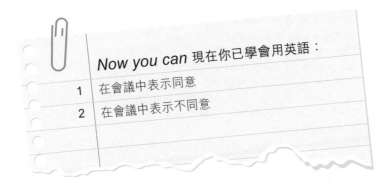

Now you can 現在你已學會用英語：

1	在會議中表示同意
2	在會議中表示不同意

23 Finding solutions in the video conference
在視像會議上尋求解決方法

總結情況 | 提出方案 | 討論可能性

Video

11
DVD

1 湯姆、黛安、約翰和凱倫繼續視像會議討論洛維和 APU 整合的問題。閱讀他們的對話和觀看短片。黛安提議了甚麼？

Diane	**So, this is the situation:** you want the Accounting department here at Lewis to integrate our IT systems into APU's. But we don't have enough people to do it quickly and, if it isn't finished before the new financial year, we'll have a problem. So, **what can we do?**
Karen	**What about** hiring extra IT people?
John	I don't think that's going to work.
Tom	I agree with you, John. IT people can be expensive and, anyway, they don't know our two companies.
Diane	That's what I think. It'll take too long to explain everything. But **what if you** send over some of your accountants to help Robert's team?
Tom	Good idea. And **how about** sending some IT specialists too?
John	Well, **we could always** see if there are some IT people here who are able to do it if that's really necessary.
Karen	But first, **why don't you** check with Robert what extra help he needs with the new system?
John	Good point, Karen. Tom, can you send over some information as to where the problem is exactly?
Tom	I'll do that today.
Diane	Excellent. And John, if we tell you who we need, will you send us your people quickly?
John	We'll do our best. This is important.

Business tip

你要尋找創新意念解決問題時，*brainstorming* 是一個好方法。

開會時，大家先分享自己的想法，然後把想法寫在白板上。所有人提供他們的意見後，與會者才一起討論。

Understanding

11
DVD

2 再看一次短片，為每題選取最合適的答案。

1 The Accounting department at Lowis Engineering

   A has too many people.

   B hires consultants.

   C needs more people to do the integration work.

2 Tom and Diane think that extra IT people

   A are expensive and need too much time to do the work.

   B will do the job well.

   C could be a good idea.

3 Karen wants to know

   A who Robert is.

   B what help Robert needs with the new systems.

   C when Tom can contact her.

4 John wants Lowis to send to APU

   A some information about the people and the problem.

   B some information about the people.

   C some information about the problem.

Key phrases

1 Summarizing the situation

So, this is the situation:	*So, to sum up:*

2 Making proposals

What about -ing ... ?	*How about -ing ... ?*
What if you ...?	*Why don't you ... ?*

3 Discussing possibilities

What can we do?	*We could always ... .*
We can (do this) or we can (do that).	

Practice

3 配對以下兩部份，組成完整句子。

1 We can send it by mail   A always stay in a hotel.

2 He could   B say to her?

3 Why doesn't   C or we can courier the package.

4 What can I   D finishing the report first?

5 What about   E she telephone him?

4 將句裏的詞語排成正確順序。

1 about / new / trainer / hiring / How /a _____?

2 could / ask / it's / important / always / him / We / if _____.

3 don't / meeting / you / arrange / Why / another _____?

4 can / situation / we / about / do / What / the _____?

5 changing / about / systems / our / What / computer _____?

5 將湯姆和羅拔・海頓的對話排成正確順序，然後聆聽 Track 67 核對答案。

67
CD

1	Tom	So, Robert, what can we do about the IT integration problem?
	Tom	No, APU says it must be this year. What else can we do?
	Robert	Of course. If this doesn't work, I'll lose my job!
	Tom	That's too expensive. How about asking people at APU to help?
	Robert	Good idea!
	Robert	We could always hire some extra people.
	Tom	Can you give me a list of the people you need?
	Robert	What if we ask APU if we can do the integration next year?

Language spotlight

第一類條件句的否定和提問形式

If it isn't finished before the new financial year, we'll have a problem.
If it's finished before the new financial year, we won't have a problem.
If we tell you who we need, will you send us your people quickly?

要令條件句轉為否定式，我們可加 not / don't / doesn't 在 if- 從句裏面，或加 not 在結果從句裏面。如果要提問題，我們可將結果從句轉成問題形式。

翻到 169 頁了解更多資料和做練習。

Speaking

6 聆聽 Track 68 的問題，然後跟着朗讀，要注意關鍵字的重音。

68
CD

1 What can we **do**?
2 What about **hiring** extra **people**?
3 What if you send some of your **accountants** to help Robert's **team**?
4 How about some IT specialists **too**?
5 Why don't you check with **Robert** what help he needs?
6 Can you send me some **information** about the problem?

7 你和你的同事安琪要為公司舉辦一個新的英語培訓課程，討論不同的可能性。在播放錄音前閱讀提示和回應，然後播放 Track 69，在咇一聲後說話。再聆聽 Track 70 比較你的對話。

69–70
CD

Angie	Well, we need to decide what to do about the English training. What do you think we can do?
You	*(Suggest sending people to the UK or Australia.)*
Angie	I think that's too expensive.
You	*(Suggest hiring an English teacher.)*
Angie	But it's difficult to know if they are good English teachers.
You	*(Suggest working with a good school.)*
Angie	Yes, that's a good idea. What should I do next?
You	*(Suggest she checks how many people want to study English.)*
Angie	Good idea!

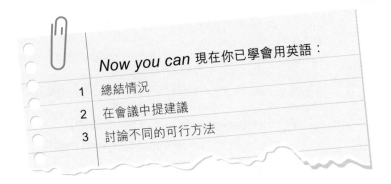

Now you can 現在你已學會用英語：

1	總結情況
2	在會議中提建議
3	討論不同的可行方法

24 Ending the video conference
結束視像會議

結束會議 | 安排新預約 | 道別

12
DVD

1 湯姆、黛安、約翰和凱倫差不多完成視像會議,閱讀他們的對話並觀看短片。他們下次的視像會議在甚麼時候?

John	So, **have we covered everything** today?
Diane	**Yes. I think that covers everything.**
John	**So to recap**, I'm going to tell the head of the Accounting department here that some of his experts must be flown to London for a few weeks.
Karen	And I'll check which of our IT specialists can be sent to you as well.
Diane	Fantastic! With this solution I really think the accounting systems will be integrated on time.
John	Great! Would it be possible to have someone arrange the hotels and security passes for our team?
Diane	No problem. My PA, Jasmine, will handle that.
John	Ah yes, Jasmine! So, **when should we next meet?**
Tom	**When is a good time for you?**
John	OK, **let me check my schedule.** Ah, how is this time Thursday next week for you?
Diane	**That's good for me.**
Tom	Me, too.

Karen	And me!
Tom	Should I send invitations and set up the video conference?
John	Ah, yes, thanks Tom, that would be great. So, we'll be in touch soon. And next week, Diane, we must discuss the senior management conference.
Diane	Excellent idea. I look forward to it. Bye then!
Tom	**See you next week then.**
Karen	Bye
John	Take care!

Business tip

結束會議之前，最好重溫要點一次，以肯定每個人明白同意了甚麼，並知道自己需要跟進的事。

Understanding

12
DVD

2 再看一次短片，改正湯姆在會議中寫下的一些行動。

- John will ask for accounting specialists to fly to London.
- Diane will look for IT specialists.
- Jasmine will arrange hotels and security passes for them.
- I will set up video conference for Tuesday next week.

Key phrases

1 Ending a meeting

Have we covered everything today?	*I think that covers everything.*
So to recap, ...	

2 Arranging a new appointment

When should we next meet?	*When is a good time for you?*
Let me check my schedule.	*Does XYZ suit you?*
That's good for me!	*See you next week then.*

3 從方框選取合適詞語完成句子。

covered	her	include	See	suit	think	When

1 When is a good time for _____?
2 Does Friday two pm _____ you?
3 I _____ that covers everything.
4 _____ should we next meet?
5 Have we _____ everything?
6 _____ you tomorrow.

4 將句裏的詞語排成正確順序。

1 Monday / you / next / afternoon / Does / week / suit _____?
2 me / my / schedule / Let / check / month / for / next _____.
3 good / time's / for / That / us _____.
4 to / our / recap / discussions / So / today _____, ...
5 is / time / a / for / Mr / When / good / Holden _____?

5 按以下情況，寫出最貼切的短語或句子。

1 You want to check the points agreed in the meeting.
   _____

2 You think that all the points have been discussed.
   _____

3 You want to arrange another meeting.
   _____

4 You want to check your schedule.
   _____

5 You want to suggest a time.
   _____

6 Say that a time is suitable for you.
   _____

Language spotlight

被動式

Some experts <u>must be flown</u> to London.
I'll check which of our IT specialists <u>can be sent</u>.
I think the accounting systems <u>will be integrated</u> on time.

當行動比進行動作的人更有趣或更重要，我們用被動式。

翻到 175 頁了解更多資料和做練習。

Speaking

71
CD

6 當你想表達你喜歡某個主意時，語氣聽起來熱情很重要。聆聽 Track 71，
然後跟着朗讀這些詞語或短語。

1　That's good!

2　Fantastic!

3　Great!

4　Excellent idea!

72–73
CD

7 你和你的同事快要完成一個會議。在播放錄音前閱讀提示和回應，然後
播放 Track 72，在嗶一聲後説話。再聆聽 Track 73 比較你的對話。

Tony	Well, have we covered everything?
You	*(Yes / think / cover / everything.)*
Tony	So, to recap. My team must be trained to use the new system. And the trainers can be provided by this company, xSoft. Is that correct?
You	*(Yes. When / next / meet?)*
Tony	Let me check my schedule.
You	*(Tuesday / four o'clock?)*
Tony	Sorry, no. How about two o'clock?
You	*(Good)*
Tony	Great. Shall we go for a coffee? I need one!
You	*(Agree)*

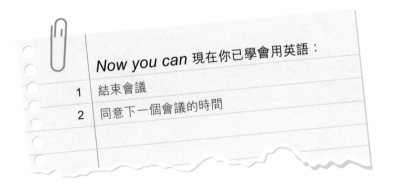

Now you can 現在你已學會用英語：

1　結束會議

2　同意下一個會議的時間

Unit 1   Back in the office 回到公司

Conversation

1 Diane wants Tom to come to a meeting with John Carter and Karen Taylor from APU.

See page 8 for video script.

Understanding

2

1 Yes, he does. Tom knows Cathy and Julia.
2 Yes, he did. Tom enjoyed his weekend.
3 Jasmine is making photocopies for Tom.
4 Tom is changing the agenda.
5 Cathy telephones Tom.
6 They will meet John Carter and Karen Taylor in the board room.

Practice

3

1 C   2 E   3 D   4 B   5 A

4

1 Hello! / Hi!
2 Good weekend?
3 How was your weekend?
4 Good morning!
5 How are you?

5

Tom	Morning, Roberta.
Roberta	Morning, Tom. How are you?
Tom	Fine, thanks. Good weekend?
Roberta	Great, thanks. I played golf on Sunday. How was your weekend?
Tom	Very nice, thanks.

6

See page 11 for audio script.

Speaking

7

Model conversation

Colin	Morning!
You	*Morning, Colin!*
Colin	How are you?
You	*Fine, thanks, and you?*
Colin	Very well, thanks. Good weekend?
You	*Great thanks! How was your vacation?*
Colin	Very good, thanks. We went to France. What are you working on at the moment?
You	*Oh, I'm practising my English.*
Colin	That's a good idea!
You	*What are you doing?*
Colin	Oh, I'm waiting for some coffee.

Unit 2　Visitors to the company
來公司的訪客

Conversation

1　Diane hasn't met Karen Taylor before.

See page 12 for video script.

Understanding

2

1	A		2	C		3	B

Practice

3

1	E	2	D	3	A	4	C	5	B

4

1　to / too
2　of / at
3　for
4　to
5　in

5

Jasmine	Hi, John, good to see you again!
John	Hello, Jasmine, good to see you again, too.
Jasmine	Can I introduce my colleague, Julia?
John	Pleased to meet you.
Julia	Pleased to meet you, too.
John	What do you do, Julia?
Julia	I'm Mr Fisher's personal assistant.

6

See page 15 for audio script.

Speaking

7

Model conversation

You	*Jenny! Good to see you again!*
Jenny	Oh, hello! Good to see you again too! Can I introduce my colleague, Alex?
You	*Hello, Alex, nice to meet you!*
Alex	Nice to meet you too.
You	*What do you do, Alex?*
Alex	Oh I'm responsible for sales and marketing. What about you?
You	*I'm a sales manager.*
Alex	Interesting.
You	*Let me introduce you to my colleague, Tom.*
Jenny, Alex, Tom	Hi … hello … pleased to meet you both.
You	*Let me give you my card.*
Alex:	Oh, thanks. Here's mine!

Answer key / Audio script

Unit 3 Down to business 直入正題

Conversation

1 Tom is going to help Karen from APU with integrating Lewis into APU.

See page 16 for video script.

Understanding

2

1 True.
2 False, she deal with systems.
3 True.
4 False, Karen does want Tom's help.
5 True.
6 False, John does want to make a phone call.

Practice

3

1 would
2 mind
3 need
4 coming
5 Could
6 by

4

1 Would you mind if we open the windows?
2 The boss really needs you to give him a call.
3 Let's start by checking some information.
4 She'd like you to come to the meeting.
5 Could you check my reservation?
6 Thank you all for coming to this meeting this morning.

5

Sample answers

1 James, I want you to do something for me.

2 Would you mind if I turn on the light?
3 Could you give me some paper?
4 The company really needs you to help me with this project.
5 When that's finished, I'd like you to join my team.

Speaking

6

See page 19 for audio script.

7

Model conversation

You	OK, thank you for coming to this meeting.
Helen + Colin	OK, good.
You	Now, I really need you to do some things for me.
Helen + Colin	Fine. No problem.
You	Colin, could you check the project costs for me?
Colin	Sure. Can I get the figures from you tomorrow morning?
You	I'm not going to be in the office tomorrow morning. Can you come to my office after the meeting?
Colin	Of course.
You	Helen, I'd like you to visit the factory with me.
Helen	Great! When?
You	I'm going to check it on Monday next week.
Helen	OK.
You	Finally, could you send me all your reports by Friday lunch time?
Helen + Colin	Sure. No problem.

Unit 4　The presentation 匯報

Conversation

1　France [Strasbourg], Korea [Seoul] and the USA [Houston]

See page 20 for video script.

Understanding

2

1	C	2	A	3	B

Practice

3

1	D	2	A	3	B	4	C

4

1　like
2　firstly
3　secondly
4　all
5　After
6　then

5

Suggested answers

1　I would like to tell you something about my company.
2　Firstly, the size.
3　Secondly, the products.
4　So first of all, we have offices in more than 50 countries and 200,000 people work for us.
5　After we opened offices in Korea in 2008, we then built factories in Vietnam.

6

See page 23 for audio script.

Speaking

7

Model presentation

> I'd like to tell you about the new payment terms, first the change in terms and second the reasons for the change.
>
> So, first of all, the change in terms. From January 1st the payment terms will be 90 days not 60 days.
>
> Second, the reason for the change in terms. Ninety days is what our customers require.

Unit 5 Questions and answers at the presentation
匯報中的問答

1 Diane was a sales manager, responsible for Asia.

See page 24 for video script.

Understanding

2

1 False, she worked in Seoul, too.
2 True
3 False, Lee Ji-Sung was responsible for the xRoot project in Asia.
4 True
5 False, he says it went fast.

Practice

3

1 glad
2 understand
3 good
4 I
5 me

4

1 Do you have any questions about the presentation?
2 I'm not sure about that point.
3 Let me think about that question.
4 Thank you for asking that question.

5

Suggested answers

1 Do you have any questions?
2 Sorry, I don't understand your question.
3 I'm not sure about that.
4 Let me think

Speaking

6

See page 26 for audio script.

7

Model conversation

You	*Do you have any questions?*
C1	Yes. How much time did you need to develop your product?
You	*Sorry, I don't understand your question.*
C1	I mean, how long did it take from start to finish?
You	*I see. It took nine months.*
C2	Was the product tested in Taiwan?
You	*I'm not quite sure about that. Can I send you the answer by email?*
C2	Of course. How many people worked on the project?
You	*I'm glad you asked that question. It wasn't many, only six engineers.*

8

Model conversation

You	*Were you responsible for the project?*
Supplier	Yes, I was.
You	*How much did the project cost?*
Supplier	I'm afraid I can't tell you that information.
You	*I understand. Where did the six engineers work?*
Supplier	They worked as a team in the UK.
You	*Thanks. That's all.*
Supplier	My pleasure.

Unit 6 Closing the meeting 結束會議

Conversation

1 Tom promises to send Karen a list of the IT systems in Lowis.

See page 28 for video script.

Understanding

2

1 Tom and Karen will work on the integration project ~~part time~~. *full time*

2 John and Diane will have a meeting every ~~month~~. *week*

3 On ~~Friday~~ Tom will send the list of IT systems to Karen. *Wednesday*

4 Diane ordered some ~~pizzas~~ for lunch. *sandwiches*

5 Karen doesn't eat ~~fruit~~. *meat*

Practice

3

1 C 2 A 3 B 4 E 5 D

4

1 I think that's enough for today.

2 Please help yourself to something to eat.

3 Could you pass me some orange juice, John?

4 Would you like some fruit?

5

Suggested answers

1 Could you pass me a [bottle of] mineral water?

2 Are you OK with that?

3 Would you like some cheese?

4 I'm afraid I don't eat meat.

5 Have some mango. It's delicious!

6

See page 31 for audio script.

Speaking

7

Model conversation

You	I think that's enough for today.
Cindy	That's good.
You	So, I ordered some refreshments. I hope you're hungry!
Cindy	Yes. Very.
You	Please help yourself!
Cindy	Mm, it looks great!
You	Could you pass me an orange juice, please?
Cindy	Here you are. Um ... is that beef in the sandwich? I'm afraid I don't eat meat!
You	Would you like a cheese salad sandwich?
Cindy	Oh, thanks! Sorry to be difficult!
You	No problem. I can't eat fish myself.

Unit 7 On the phone to Australia
打電話到澳洲

Telephone call

1 Karen is on a business trip.

See page 32 for video script.

Understanding

2

1 C **2** B **3** C **4** A

Practice

3

1 E **2** A **3** B **4** C **5** D

4

1 Can you put me through to Julia, please?

2 I'm afraid he's in a meeting at the moment.

3 Can I speak to Jasmine Goodman, please?

4 I'll write him an email.

5 Hi, this is David Knopf from xRoot Software.

5

Suggested answers

1 (Your name) speaking.

2 I'm afraid he / she is in a meeting.

3 Hold the line, please.

4 I'm sorry but his line's busy.

5 Can I take a message?

6

See page 35 for audio script.

Speaking

7

Model conversation

Jodie	Compex Incorporated, Jodie King speaking. How can I help you?
You	*Hello, this Michelle Blanc from Tapette. Can I speak to Frank Linker, please?*
Jodie	I'm afraid he's in a meeting.
You	*OK. I'll send him an email. Could you put me through to Susie Goh?*
Jodie	I'm sorry but her line's busy at the moment. Can I take a message?
You	*Don't worry, I'll call back later. Thank you very much for your assistance. Goodbye!*
Jodie	Goodbye!

Unit 8   Emailing Australia 電郵到澳洲

Email

1   Tom suggests a telephone conference call.

Understanding

2

1   False, he emailed her. He spoke to Kim.
2   False, she is on a business trip.
3   False, Tom wants to organize a telephone conference.
4   False, she is back in the office on Friday.
5   True.

Practice

3

1   With regard to **your** project in India ….
2   I think it's a good idea if we ….
3   I tried to speak to you this morning **but** you were in a meeting.
4   I suggest that **we** meet as soon as possible.
5   Could you let **me** know if that's convenient?
6   I'm out of the office **until** Monday.

4

Dear Ms Goodman

I tried to call you this afternoon but you were in a meeting.

With regard to our meeting tomorrow, I think it's a good idea if we also discuss the project costs. I suggest that I invite our accountant, Gordon King, to the meeting.

I look forward to seeing you tomorrow.

Best wishes

Priti Makesch

5

Suggested answers

1   Bernhard
2   this morning
3   visiting a customer
4   project
5   visit you next week
6   bring my colleague
7   James

Writing

6

Model email

Dear Amy

I tried to return your call but I heard you are flying to China.

With regard to your questions, I think it's a good idea if we speak on the phone. I suggest I call you tomorrow at 6pm Beijing time. Can you send me the telephone number of the hotel?

I look forward to speaking to you tomorrow.

Best wishes

Pascale

7

Model out-of-office message

I am away from Model out-of-office message _____ to _____ on vacation. Please contact Susan Smith on smith@XYZ.com with any enquiries.

Answer key / Audio script

Unit 9 Starting the telephone conference call
開始電話會議

Telephone conference call

1 Tom is at home.

See page 40 for audio script.

Understanding

2

1 Tom is working from home today.

2 Because it is an international company and needs different systems for different countries.

3 It only takes two days.

Practice

3

1	F	2	C	3	G	4	E
5	B	6	D	7	A		

4

1 Diane works from home on Mondays.

2 I'm sitting here with Kim and Bernadette.

3 Can you tell me how much it costs?

4 Do you know how many offices you have worldwide?

5

John	John Carter here. Hello, Mr Park.
Mr Park	Good evening, Mr Carter.
John	My colleague Karen Taylor will call in in a moment from home.
Karen	Hello John, hello Mr Park. Sorry I'm late.
Mr Park	No problem, Ms Taylor.
John	Good. Well, let's start. Can you tell us how much time you have for us today?
Mr Park	As much time as you want, Mr Carter.
John	Great! Well, first of all, we need to know how much your new products will cost?

Speaking

6

See page 43 for audio script.

7

Model conversation

Recorded voice	Another caller is entering the conference.
You	*Hello, it's Paul here.*
Jun + Pascale	Hi, Jun here. Hello, this is Pascale!
You	*Hi there. Sorry I'm late.*
Pascale	That's OK!
You	*I'm working from home today. How much time do we need?*
Jun	As much time as you want. Well, let's start. Can you tell us how many people you have for this project in your office?
You	*Not many, only a few. How many people do you have, Pascale?*
Pascale	Oh it's the same for me. Only a few.
You	*Can you tell me how many people you need?*
Pascale	I think another five at least!

Unit 10   Ending the telephone conference call
結束電話會議

Telephone conference call

1   Tom is staying one night in Portsmouth.

See page 44 for video script.

Understanding

2

1   False, Karen is flying to London next week.
2   True
3   False, Tom is visiting a customer, not a supplier.
4   False, He says he's not sure if that's a really good idea.
5   True

Practice

3

1   Speak
2   lunchtime
3   Mr Carter's
4   seeing
5   Tuesday

4

1	D	2	A	3	B	4	C

5

1	John	I just want to let you know. I'm flying to Seoul ~~last~~ week. *next*
2	Mr Park	Oh, let ~~my~~ check my schedule. *me*
3	John:	How ~~do~~ Wednesday look? *does*
4	Mr Park	Hmm, not too bad. What about ~~on~~ 10 o'clock in your hotel? *at*

5	John	That's fine. I'm ~~have~~ a meeting at the APU office after lunch. *having*
6	Mr Park	OK. So, 10 o'clock Wednesday. Nice speaking ~~at~~ you, John. *to*
7	John	Yes. ~~He's~~ looking forward to seeing you soon! *I'm*

Speaking

6

See page 47 for audio script.

7

Model conversation

Jun	Well, I think ...and I think a meeting is a very good idea.
You	*I'm flying to Tokyo next week.*
Jun	Let me check my schedule.
You	*How does Tuesday afternoon look?*
Jun	Oh, I'm sorry, I'm visiting a supplier outside Tokyo on Tuesday.
You	*Well, I'm staying in Tokyo until Friday.*
Jun	Oh, very good. Then I have a chance to see you on Thursday morning.
You	*Hmm, I'm meeting somebody at my hotel in the morning. What about your plans for Thursday afternoon?*
Jun	Yes, that's fine. Is three o'clock OK?
You	*That's an excellent idea.*
Jun	Great. Well, it was good to speak to you, Karl. See you next week!
You	*I'm looking forward to it, Jun. Goodbye.*
Jun	Goodbye!

Unit 11   Making plans by email
通過電郵商定計劃

Email

1 Karen suggests that she comes to Tom's meeting on Monday morning with the Lowis sales team.

Understanding

2

1 Karen wants to come to Tom's meeting.

2 The sales people don't use the APU system yet.

3 Tom and Karen are driving to Portsmouth.

4 Karen must meet Peter King on Tuesday morning.

5 Karen has to check the servers for John.

6 Karen has to fly back to Sydney on Friday.

Practice

3

1 E   2 C   3 B   4 A   5 D

4

1 Would you mind speaking to Jun and Pascale?

2 What's your opinion on the problem?

3 Do you think you could send me the report?

4 Shall we send the figures to the project manager?

5 If this is OK for you, we can work together.

6 Why don't we have a meeting on Wednesday?

5

1 Why don't

2 we could

3 do you feel about this

4 this is OK with

5 must

6 you mind

Writing

6

Model email

Dear Pascale

I'm visiting Paris next week for a sales conference. Why don't we have a meeting to discuss the project progress? If you're OK with this, perhaps we could go for lunch. How do you feel about this?

Shall we meet at your office at one o'clock? Would you mind making reservations in a restaurant?

Best regards

Jun

Unit 12   Telephone small talk
電話閒談

Telephone call

1   John's suggestion is that Tom visit Australia for a week.

See page 52 for audio script.

Understanding

2

1   A   2   B   3   C

Practice

3

1   What are … .
2   I have to check … .
3   Did you … .
4   I was wondering if you … .
5   When is a good … .

4

1   It's raining here.
2   What are you doing this evening?
3   What's work like at the moment?
4   Did you see the football last night?
5   When is a good time for you?

5

Karen	How's the weather in London?
Peter	It's raining here.
Karen	Too bad! Listen, I'm visiting the UK next week. I was wondering if we could have a meeting some time?
Peter	Well, on Tuesday perhaps.
Karen	Sure. When's a good time for you? The afternoon maybe?
Peter	Hmm, I have to check my schedule. Oh, I'm sorry but the afternoon's no good.
Karen	Well, what are you doing on Tuesday morning?
Peter	Tuesday morning is fine.

Speaking

6

See page 55 for audio script.

7

Model conversation

You	Hello, Colin. How's the weather?
Colin	Oh, hello! It's raining here!
You	Too bad! What's work like at the moment?
Colin	Very busy!
You	I'm visiting Manchester next week. I was wondering if I could visit you.
Colin	Well, next week is busy, but I'm sure it's possible.
You	What are your plans for Thursday?
Colin	Hmm, not so good. What are you doing on Wednesday?
You	I have to check my schedule.
Colin	No problem.
You	When is a good time for you on Wednesday?
Colin	Wednesday morning is fine.

Answer key / Audio script

Unit 13 Arranging the business trip
安排出差

Email

1 He plans to stay eight nights.

Understanding

2

1 Tom wants APU to book a hotel room for him.

2 Tom suggests a telephone conference and inviting Robert Holden and Peter King to the telco.

3 John thinks a telco is a good idea but that it is not necessary to invite Robert Holden and Peter King.

4 Pia Levene, John's assistant, will arrange the hotel room.

5 To do something on the Saturday night.

Practice

3

1	for	2	if	3	As
4	for	5	ending		

4

1 Let me know if that date is OK.

2 The week ending 25 June is good for me.

3 Following our meeting this afternoon, here are my notes.

4 Thanks for your phone call this morning.

5 Would it be possible for you to reserve a meeting room?

5

1 following – Following

2 Febuary - February

3 bee – be

4 arrives – arrive / will arrive

5 regard – regards

6 late – let

7 best – Best

Writing

6

Model email

Dear Mr Murray

Thank you for your email yesterday. I think your services sound very interesting. Would it be possible for you to visit my office next month on 12 June?

If you want, my assistant will reserve a hotel for you.

Please let me know if this is possible.

Best regards

…

7

Model email

Dear …

Thank you very much for your reply to my email. 12 June in the morning is good for me. What time would you like to meet? Thanks for your offer to reserve a hotel room but that is not necessary.

Unit 14 Priorities for the business trip
出差行程的先後緩急

Email

1 Karen is the first person on the conference call.

See page 60 for audio script.

Understanding

2

1 data centre
2 data security
3 developments
4 accounting
5 important

Practice

3

1 D   2 A   3 B   4 C

4

1 that
2 to
3 second / secondly
4 of
5 important

5

(Example answers)

1 check your emails
2 plan your schedule
3 answer your emails
4 go to lunch!

6

See page 63 for audio script.

Speaking

7

Model conversation

Jun	So I'm coming to visit you and other people next month. What topics should we discuss?
You	**First,** we can discuss the project schedule.
Jun	Good idea. What next?
You	**Second,** we have to check the project costs.
Jun	I agree. And after that?
You	After that, we **need to** talk about the problems with the consultants.
Jun	Yes, that is a big problem. Anything else?
You	Finally, we **have to** go out for **dinner**.
Jun	That's a very good idea!

Answer key / Audio script

Unit 15 Dealing with questions in the conference call
處理電話會議的提問

Telephone conference call

Diane suggests a conference for the senior management level of Lowis and APU. At first John is not sure about the suggestion but in the end he thinks it is a good idea.

See page 64 for audio script.

Understanding

2

1 B   2 C   3 C

Practice

3

1 D   2 A   3 B   4 C

4

1 I'm sorry but could you repeat that last word?
2 What do you mean by 'delayed'?
3 But I don't understand why it's a problem.
4 Can you give me an example of this?

5

1 I'm afraid I don't / is it
2 you give an
3 there a reason why
4 I'm / Could you repeat
5 But I don't / what

6

See page 67 for audio script.

Speaking

7

Model conversation

Supplier	Then there was a strike at the factory.
You	*I'm sorry. Could you repeat that?*
Supplier	There was a strike.
You	*I'm afraid I don't understand the word.*
Supplier	Oh, I see. A strike. The workers stopped working.
You	*Oh, I understand now. Is there a reason why they had a strike now?*
Supplier	Well, they weren't happy with the new terms and conditions.
You	*Can you give me an example?*
Supplier	Well, first the workers wanted more money.
You	*Can you repeat that? I'm afraid I didn't hear what you said?*
Supplier	The workers wanted more money.

Unit 16 Written invitations 撰寫邀請

1 The conference will be in London on January 10. Joe Smith is not sure at the moment if he can attend. He needs to change his plans.

Understanding

2

1 False, the email is sent to senior managers at APU and Lowis.
2 True
3 False, Diane and John want people to email them with their answer.
4 False, the information about the conference will be sent when they answer the email.
5 True
6 False, Joe is not sure at the moment.

Practice

3

1 We are pleased **to** invite you to the opening of our new offices in Penang.
2 We would be grateful **if** you inform us about your plans.
3 We **look** forward to welcoming you to our new offices in the near future.
4 This occasion **will** be an opportunity to meet senior managers.

4

1 ~~dade~~. date
2 ~~plaice~~ place
3 ~~next~~ near
4 ~~Truly~~ truly

5

1 We are pleased to invite you to our sales conference on September 13.
2 The event will take place in the Tower Hotel.
3 The occasion will be an opportunity for you to meet our staff.
4 Yours truly

Writing

6

Model email

Dear Colleagues

We are pleased to invite you to the opening of our Munich factory. The event will take place on April 4 at 10.00 am. This occasion will be an opportunity to see our new equipment in action.

We would be grateful if you could reply before March 1. As soon as we receive your reply, we will send details of the event, the location and the hotel.

We look forward to meeting you at our factory opening.

Yours truly

James Scott

7

Model email

Dear James

Thank you very much for your invitation to the opening of the Munich factory.

At the moment I'm not sure if I can be there. As soon as I know, I will get back to you to say if I can attend.

With thanks

Unit 17 Business trip details
出差詳情

Email

1 Pia is writing to Tom to give him information about his hotel in Sydney and other arrangements.

Understanding

2

1 The hotel will send a limousine to meet Tom.

2 Pia wants Tom to send flight details.

3 Tom can check the hotel facilities on the hotel's website.

4 John is taking Tom to the opera house to see *Carmen*.

Practice

3

1 B   **2** E   **3** A   **4** C   **5** D

4

1 Jasmine will arrange for the documents to be photocopied.

2 I would like to confirm your landing time at Singapore Airport.

3 You can find more details in the attached document.

4 Let me introduce myself – my name's Jasmine Goodman.

5 Please call me if you have any problems.

5

1 ~~my~~ me

2 ~~will~~ would

3 ~~four~~ for

4 ~~are~~ is

5 ~~detail~~ detailed

6 ~~cheque~~ check

7 ~~has~~ have

Writing

6

Model email

Dear Ms Binders

Let me introduce myself – I am ....'s assistant, and **I would like to confirm** your hotel arrangements.

I have booked you into the Harunami Hotel for three nights (March 23-26). The hotel has sent me a confirmation code for your reservation, HH23MAR211.

For further information about the hotel, **please check their website** here: **www.harunami_hotel.com**

... has reserved a table in a restaurant for March 24. She / He will meet you in the hotel lobby at 7.00 pm.

Please contact me if you have any questions.

Yours sincerely

XYZ

Unit 18　Changes to the schedule
更改日程

Email

1 Tom is staying for eight days in Australia.

See page 76 for audio script.

Understanding

2

1 Tom Field – Lowis Engineering

2 Wants to change ~~hotel~~ *schedule*

3 Arrive Sydney Oct 16

4 Hire car Oct 19

5 ~~Visited Sydney already~~ *Hasn't visited Sydney already*

6 Send ~~letter~~ confirming details *email*

Practice

3

1 D　2 C　3 B　4 A　5 E

4

1 can

2 ask

3 Would

4 kind

5 lot

5

Jasmine	Jasmine Goodman, Lowis Engineering London. How can I help you?
Eva	Hello. This is Eva Schmidt here. I wonder if I could ask you a favour.
Jasmine	Of course, Ms Schmidt. What can I do for you?

Eva	Well, you booked me a room at the Tower Hotel for three nights. Would you mind changing the reservation to only one night? For the last two nights I'm going to stay with friends.
Jasmine	No problem. So you only want a room for October 31st?
Eva	That's right.
Jasmine	Fine. Would you like me to organize for you to be met at the airport when you arrive?
Eva	No, it's OK, thank you. I'll take the underground. But thanks a lot for your help with the arrangements.
Jasmine	My pleasure!

Speaking

6

See page 79 for audio script.

7

Model email

Frank	Frank Richards speaking.
You	*Hello, it's Jim Levy here. I wonder if I could ask you a favour.*
Frank	Of course. What can I do for you?
You	*I wanted to ask if you could change my meeting time with Mr Ho.*
Frank	I'm sure we can find a time. When is convenient?
You	*Would ten o'clock on Tuesday be possible?*
Frank	Let me see … well, I need to change another appointment of Mr Ho's, but that's not a problem.
You	*Oh, that's great. Thanks a lot for your help with the arrangements!*
Frank	My pleasure!

Unit 19 Welcome back to the office
歡迎回到公司

Video

1 Tom didn't like the stop at Moscow.

See page 80 for video script.

Understanding

2

1 C   2 A   3 A

Practice

3

1 It's nice / good
2 What was
3 Did you do
4 Good to see
5 What did you
6 It's nice / good to have you back.

4

1 What did you get up to in Paris?
2 What was the weather like when you were in Seattle?
3 Did she do any sightseeing when she was there?
4 Is everything going well in Shanghai?
5 Good to see you again!

5

Robert	Hi, Jasmine. Good to see you again!
Jasmine	Hello, Robert. Nice to have you back! Good flight?
Robert	No, it was awful. But Beijing was great!
Jasmine	Really? Did you do any sightseeing?
Robert	Some. I saw the Great Wall.

Jasmine	Fantastic! What was the weather like?
Robert	Oh, great. On the hottest day it was about 35 degrees!
Jasmine	Lucky you. It rained here.
Robert	Yes, Diane told me. But still, it's nice to be back!

Speaking

6

See page 83 for audio script.

7

Model conversation

Cathy	Hello! Good to see you again.
You	*Hi, Cathy! It's nice to have you back again. Did you have a good flight?*
Cathy	Yes, it was fine.
You	*Is everything OK in the New York office?*
Cathy	Yes. I had a very interesting time.
You	*Did you do any sightseeing?*
Cathy	No, not really. But I did go shopping.
You	*Lucky you! What did you buy?*
Cathy	Well, I went to Bloomingdale's because I've always wanted to go there. I bought a bag.
You	*Great! What was the weather like?*
Cathy	Oh, it was good. Sunny and warm.
You	*It was very cold here.*
Cathy	Oh, dear.

Unit 20 The project review 檢討項目

Video

1 The integration of the accounting systems is behind schedule.

See page 84 for video script.

Understanding

2

1 False, John and Karen are worried about the project. They think it's going too slow.

2 True

3 True

4 False, no, they aren't. Not yet.

5 True

Practice

3

1 E **2** C **3** A **4** B **5** D

4

Suggested answers

1 Can you show me the figures for July?

2 I don't understand why it takes so long.

3 When did you speak to him?

4 Have you written the email yet?

5 When will you finish the job?

5

Suggested answers

1 Let's look at the project schedule.

2 Here we can see the problems with the costs.

3 Moving on to the question of quality.

4 The next slide shows the next steps.

Speaking

6

See page 87 for audio script.

7

Model conversation

Team member	So let's look at the project status then. Here we can see the costs so far.
You	*Can you show me the time schedule?*
Team member	Yes, well the next slide shows the detailed schedule for the system integration and the training programme.
You	*Have you started the training programme yet?*
Team member	No, we haven't started it yet.
You	*I don't understand why not.*
Team member	Well, the equipment isn't ready yet.
You	*When will it be ready?*
Team member	It'll be ready by the end of this week. But we've finished the software update already.
You	*Good! When did you do that?*
Team member	That was on Friday last week.

Answer key / Audio script

Unit 21 Starting the video conference 開始視像會議

1 No, they can't solve the problem.

See page 88 for video script.

Understanding

2

1 Karen and John have a problem.
2 They can't make their video conferencing equipment work.
3 They call a technician.

Practice

3

1 keep
2 click
3 wrong
4 on
5 trouble

4

1 We're having trouble with the server.
2 I think we need to call the help desk.
3 Just a moment, please.
4 When I open my email account, my computer crashes.
5 The telephone doesn't seem to be working.

5

1 My system has crashed.
2 I'm having problems opening my email account.
3 There seems to be something wrong with the printer.
4 The internet doesn't seem to be working.
5 Sorry to keep you waiting.

Speaking

6

See page 91 for audio script.

7

Model conversation

Help desk	How can I help you?
You	*There seems to be something wrong with my computer.*
Help desk	OK. What's the matter?
You	*I seem to be having problems with the screen.*
Help desk	OK. Have you tried to reboot your computer?
You	*When I click on the restart icon, nothing happens.*
Help desk	Have you tried to turn off the computer and then restart?
You	*Hold on a moment.*
Help desk	No problem.
You	*Sorry to keep you waiting. No, I think I need a technician.*
Help desk	OK, I'll come up to your office.
You	*Thanks a lot.*

Unit 22　Discussing problems in the video conference
在視像會議上討論問題

Video

1 Diane doesn't want to put pressure on the accounting department.

See page 92 for video script.

Understanding

2

1 False, Karen and John think the integration of the accounting department is going badly.

2 True

3 False, Diane disagrees with Karen.

4 False, the accounting team doesn't have enough people.

5 True

Practice

3

1 B　2 D　3 E　4 A　5 C

4

1 sure

2 sorry

3 not

4 absolutely

5 so

5

Fiona	We need to open a new office in Moscow for our Russian customers. What do you think?
Simon	Yes, I agree. We need to be close to our customers.
Tom	Yes, but at the moment we don't have any customers there, do we?
Simon	I don't agree. We have some business with Vladivoil. We need to increase that.
Fiona	I think so too. Russia is the next big market.
Tom	I'm sorry but I don't think it's a good idea. It's vey expensive to open an office in Russia.
Simon	We need to remember the costs. You're quite right. Perhaps we should close the office in Sydney and then open an office in Moscow.
Fiona	I'm sorry but I don't think that's a good idea, Simon!

Speaking

6

See page 94 for audio script.

7

Model conversation

Dale	Well, the next point on the agenda is IT strategy. We need to decide what to do next about our business management system.
You	*You're absolutely right.*
Dale	In the US we think we need to update our business management system.
You	*I'm sorry but I don't think that's a good idea. The present system works fine.*
Dale	But the new system is really easy to use!
You	*Well, I don't agree. I think the new system has problems.*
Dale	Well, the present system does work well.
You	*I think so, too.*
Dale	But the new system is much faster.*
You	*Look, let's continue the discussion at lunch.*
Dale	Good idea!

Collins Workplace English (Business Interaction) **125**

Unit 23 Finding solutions in the video conference
在視像會議上尋求解決方法

Video

1 Diane suggests that APU send people to help the Accounting department at Lowis with the system integration.

See page 96 for video script.

Understanding

2

1 C   2 A   3 B   4 C

Practice

3

1 C   2 A   3 E   4 B   5 D

4

1 How about hiring a new trainer?

2 We could always ask him if it's important.

3 Why don't you arrange another meeting?

4 What can we do about the situation?

5 What about changing our computer systems?

5

Tom	So, Robert, what can we do about the IT integration problem?
Robert	What if we ask APU if we can do the integration next year?
Tom	No, APU says it must be this year. What else can we do?
Robert	We could always hire some extra people.
Tom	That's too expensive. How about asking people at APU to help?
Robert	Good idea!
Tom	Can you give me a list of the people you need?
Robert	Of course. If this doesn't work, I'll lose my job!

Speaking

6

See page 99 for audio script.

7

Model conversation

Angie	Well, we need to decide what to do about the English training next year. What do you think we can do?
You	*How about sending people to the UK or Australia?*
Angie	I think that's too expensive.
You	*Well, why don't we hire an English teacher?*
Angie	But it's difficult to know if they are good English teachers.
You	*We could always work together with a good school.*
Angie	Yes, that's a good idea. What should I do next?
You	*What about checking how many people want to study English?*
Angie	Good idea!

Unit 24 Ending the video conference
結束視像會議

Video

1 Their next video conference is the same time Thursday next week.

See page 100 for video script.

Understanding

2

- *John will ask for accounting specialists to fly to London.*
- *~~Diane~~ Karen will look for IT specialists.*
- *~~Karen~~ Jasmine will arrange hotels and security passes for team.*
- *I will set up videoconference for ~~Tuesday~~ Thursday next week.*

Practice

3

1 her
2 suit
3 think
4 When
5 covered
6 See

4

1 Does Monday afternoon next week suit you?
2 Let me check my schedule for next month.
3 That time's good for us.
4 So to recap our discussions today.
5 When is a good time for Mr Holden?

5

1 So let me recap, …
2 I think that covers everything.
3 When should we next meet?
4 Let me check my schedule.
5 Does Tuesday suit you?
6 That's good for me!

Speaking

6

See page 104 for audio script.

7

Model conversation

Tony	Well, have we covered everything?
You	*Yes, I think that covers everything.*
Tony	So to recap, my team must be trained to use the new system. And the trainers can be provided by this company, xSoft. Is that correct?
You	*Yes, that's right. When should we have our next meeting?*
Tony	Let me check my schedule.
You	*Does Tuesday at four o'clock suit you?*
Tony	Sorry, no. How about two o'clock?
You	*That's good for me.*
Tony	Great. Shall we go for a coffee? I need one!
You	*Me too. Good idea.*

Translation of conversations

1 Back in the office 回到公司

湯姆： <u>早晨</u>，凱詩！

凱詩： <u>早晨</u>，湯姆！

湯姆： <u>你好</u>，茉莉亞！

茉莉亞：<u>你好</u>，湯姆！

黛安： <u>你好，湯姆。你好嗎？</u>

湯姆： <u>你好，我很好，謝謝你。你呢？</u>

黛安： <u>非常好，謝謝。你週末過得好嗎？</u>

湯姆： <u>好，好極了，謝謝你。</u>我們昨天為愛美莉舉行了一個兒童生日派對，她有十個朋友來了。

黛安： <u>哇！</u>

湯姆： <u>那你的週末過得如何？</u>

黛安： <u>非常忙。</u>我現在每時每刻都在忙 APU 公司的收購。今天的議程準備好了嗎？

湯姆： 我想準備好了。茉莉正在影印你的報告，而我剛在修改今天的議程，你知道的，去那間餐廳吃午飯。

黛安： 好的。

湯姆： 湯姆·菲特。噢，你好。明白，好的，謝謝！是接待處的凱詩。她告訴我茉莉正帶着約翰·卡特和凱倫·泰萊前往會議室。

黛安： 好！那我們還等甚麼呢？走吧！

2 Visitors to the company 來公司的訪客

黛安： 約翰，你好！<u>很高興再見到你！</u>

約翰： 黛安！<u>我也很高興再見到你。</u>讓我向你介紹凱倫·泰萊。她是我們 APU 公司的資訊科技總監。

黛安： 很高興認識你。

凱倫： <u>我也很高興認識你</u>，甘迺迪女士。

黛安： 請叫我黛安。<u>讓我介紹</u>我的同事，湯姆·菲特。湯姆，約翰是 APU 公司的工程和特別項目主管。

湯姆： <u>很高興認識你們兩位，讓我給你我的名片。</u>

凱倫： <u>我也很高興認識你</u>……<u>這是我的名片</u>……。

約翰： ……這張是我的。那麼湯姆你是做甚麼的？

湯姆： 我常和黛安一起工作。我是項目主任，我負責洛維的一些大項目，我也是變革管理的專家。

凱倫： 我明白了，那你認識洛維很多不同部門的經理嗎？

湯姆： 我想是的，認識不同的人和知道他們的職責很重要。

約翰： 是的，這些對一個項目經理來說很重要。

黛安： 請坐。

3　Down to business　直入正題

黛安： 謝謝大家今天出席這個會議。首先讓我們討論將來幾個月要做甚麼事。約翰和凱倫，你們會負責洛維和 APU 公司合併 APU 公司的部份。

約翰： 説得沒錯。我會和你一起處理管理方面的問題，凱倫則負責系統方面的工作，例如資訊科技的工作。

黛安： 而湯姆，我想你和凱倫合作。

湯姆： 好的，我應該怎樣協助？

凱倫： 我希望你可以幫我了解洛維的運作，你是這方面的專家。如果沒有你的協助，你們和 APU 公司的系統整合將會很困難。

湯姆： 確實如此。

黛安： 好。湯姆，我想你對這個項目該很感興趣。

約翰： 我們真的需要你促進這次項目成功。

黛安： 正是。現在讓我們看看洛維現時的情況。湯姆，你可以在我開投影機時，幫我派講義給約翰和凱倫嗎？

約翰： 你會否介意我在你準備時打個簡短電話嗎？

黛安： 沒問題。

4　The presentation　匯報

黛安： 好，我和湯姆會將洛維過去三年兩個最大的項目告訴你們。第一，是我們的會計軟件 — xRoot，我們用於處理所有的簿記。第二，是為政府做的朱柏特項目。

首先，xRoot。幾年前我們的簿記全用簡單的試算表去做。本來這樣做沒有問題，因為當時我們只在倫敦一個辦公室工作。而當我們在史特拉斯堡、首爾和侯斯頓都設了辦事處之後，我們意識到需要升級軟件。系統最初是個問題，但我們聘請了一些顧問協助我們，現在一切都運作得很順利。

凱倫： 不好意思，你們是用德菲還是蓋普的資料庫儲存數據？

湯姆： 蓋普斯，xRoot 只能用蓋普的資料庫。

黛安： 謝謝你，湯姆。

凱倫： 我明白。

黛安： 那麼，到下一個主題，湯姆會向你們介紹朱柏特項目。

湯姆： 謝謝你，黛安。我是朱柏特項目的項目經理，那是一個 £45……

Translation of conversations

5 Questions and answers at the presentation 匯報中的問答

湯姆：　好，那麼<u>你們有沒有問題</u>？

約翰：　我有問題。黛安，請問你是不是一直都在倫敦工作？

黛安：　<u>抱歉，我不明白你的問題。</u>

約翰：　我意思是你有沒有在洛維英國以外的其他辦事處工作過？

黛安：　我明白了，<u>很高興你問那條問題</u>。約翰，我曾在其他辦事處工作。在 2008 年，我是一個銷售經理，負責亞洲區事務，而當時我在首爾工作。但我在那邊不是工作了很久，大約只工作了六個月。

凱倫：　那麼你當時是 xRoot 項目在亞洲的負責人嗎？

黛安：　不是，那是我當時的上司李景松先生負責的。

約翰：　啊，對，李先生。我上星期在悉尼見過他。另外，現在的新系統要多少錢？

黛安：　<u>那是一條好問題</u>……呃……<u>我不太清楚</u>。湯姆，你知道嗎？

湯姆：　我知道，加上蓋普的顧問費，大約要六百萬元。

凱倫：　然後安裝要多長時間？

湯姆：　很快，整個項目只用了九個月。

約翰：　那真的很快！<u>湯姆，我有條問題想問你</u>：你甚麼時候開始做朱伯特的項目？

湯姆：　<u>讓我想想。</u>　項目在十二個月之前開始，我那個時候開始……

6 Closing the meeting 結束會議

黛安：　好，<u>讓我總結一下</u>：湯姆會和凱倫一起專門負責整合的項目。凱倫會向約翰報告，而湯姆負責向我報告。

約翰：　對，還有你和我。黛安，我們每星期會有一次會議或通電話以檢查項目進度。

黛安：　好的。

湯姆：　好。那麼，凱倫，我會給你列出一個我們公司科技系統的清單，讓你知道我們有些甚麼。

凱倫：　好極了！那你甚麼時候可以給我？

湯姆：　我下星期三放在你桌上。

約翰：　約翰，<u>你覺得這樣可以嗎</u>？

約翰：　可以，很好。

黛安：　好……<u>那麼今天就到這裏。</u>

約翰：　好的。

黛安：　時間剛剛好，現在，約翰，你和我半小時後會與製作部經理克里斯‧霍斯一同參觀工廠。因我們不會有時間正式吃午飯，所以我為大家叫了些<u>三文治</u>。

約翰： 謝謝。

凱倫： 好主意。

黛安： 那麼請慢用。

凱倫： 謝謝。

約翰： 看來很好吃。

黛安： 湯姆，你可以遞水給我嗎？

凱倫： 不好意思，那是雞肉嗎？抱歉，我不吃肉。

湯姆： 噢，對不起。你想要些三文治嗎？芝士、蛋和……我想那些是沙律三文治。

凱倫： 我想我吃些水果就好了，謝謝。

黛安： 好主意。吃些芒果，它們很好吃！

7 On the phone to Australia 打電話到澳洲

金： 這是金•本德。

湯姆： 你好，我是倫敦洛維工程公司的湯姆•菲特。請問我可以和凱倫•泰萊説話嗎？

金： 噢，菲特先生，你好。我是凱倫的助理，抱歉她今天不在辦公室，她出差馬來西亞了。請問我有甚麼可以幫你？

湯姆： 我明白了，你可以幫我接駁給約翰•卡特嗎？

金： 當然可以，請稍等。你好，菲特先生？但很抱歉，他正在通電話，你有留言要我幫你寫下嗎？

湯姆： 不，不用了。我之後會再打電話給他。

金： 另外，我知道凱倫每天傍晚都檢查電郵。

湯姆： 那是個好主意！我會發電郵給她，謝謝你的幫忙。

金： 還有，她會在星期五回到辦公室，所以到時候你可以找她。

湯姆： 好的，幸好知道了，非常感謝你。

金： 不客氣。

湯姆： 再見！

金： 再見！

8 Emailing Australia 電郵到澳洲

凱倫：

我今天嘗試打電話給你，但聽説你在出差。

就有關你的電郵和提問，我認為我們和黛安、約翰及其他洛維的同事一起商討是個好主意。我提議星期五英國早上八時（澳洲時間晚上六時）舉行一個電話會議。你的助理説你那時應已回到辦公室，可否讓我知道那樣安排對你是否方便？

期待很快能和你再次商談。

祝 一切安好

湯姆

我在十一月七日星期四之前不在辦公室，我會在十一月八日星期五回到辦公室，而每天傍晚我都會看電郵。

謝謝，凱倫

9 Starting the telephone conference call 開始電話會議

預設錄音： 歡迎來到敏泰電話會議服務，請輸入電話會議識別碼，然後輸入英鎊符號。 請説出你的名字。

湯姆： 湯姆‧菲特。

預設錄音： 其他參加者來到之前，你會聽到一些音樂。

預設錄音： 另一位參加者正在進入通話。

約翰： 你好，這是約翰‧卡特。你好，湯姆？

湯姆： 你好。

約翰： 凱倫現時坐在我旁邊。

凱倫： 早晨，湯姆。

湯姆： 你好，凱倫，你好，約翰。我不是在辦公室打電話過來，因我今天在家工作，但黛安很快會和羅拔‧海頓一起打電話過來。你可以問羅拔關於會計部的 xRoot 系統。

預設錄音： 另一位參加者正在進入通話。

黛安： 你好，這是黛安和羅拔。

羅拔： 大家好，抱歉我們遲了。

湯姆： 不要緊，那麼我們開始吧。凱倫，我想你有些問題想問羅拔和我。

凱倫： 是的，湯姆，謝謝你。羅拔，你可否告訴我洛維的財政戶口要用多少個不同的科技系統？

羅拔： 嗯，我們用三個系統。

凱倫： 是，但為何你們有三個科技系統？

羅拔： 因為洛維是一間國際公司，一個系統紀錄每個國家的本地數據 —— 美國、韓國或德國。第二個系統搜集全世界的數據。第三個系統預備交給管理層和稅局的數據。

凱倫： 整個過程需要多長時間？

羅拔： 不太長，兩天我們就可以準備完整的年度報告。

約翰： 那就好。羅拔，告訴我，有多少人在會計部工作？

羅拔： 只有很少，包括實習生的話……嗯……十五人。

凱倫： 對。湯姆，你可否告訴我公司的電腦伺服器需要多少空間擺放？

湯姆： 只需要很少。我們將伺服器放在地庫，大約五平方米左右。

約翰： 我明白了，黛安，你覺得……？

10 Ending the telephone conference call 結束電話會議

黛安： …… 然後我們可以和你們的電腦系統整合，縮減電腦伺服器的數量。

羅拔： 當然也可以削減開支。

約翰： 沒錯，那非常重要。凱倫，你同意嗎？

凱倫： 當然了。另外，湯姆，我只想你知道我下星期飛往倫敦。我們可以找時間開個會嗎？你星期一有甚麼計劃？

湯姆： 讓我查一查下星期的日程表。星期一早上我和銷售團隊有會議，討論你們顧客關係管理的工具。

凱倫： 那麼星期一中午怎樣？

湯姆： 嗯，讓我看看。抱歉，不行。之後我要駕車到樸茨茅斯，拜訪我們最大的客戶，跟他們說我們公司的變動。

凱倫： 我能和你一起去嗎？那我就有機會見你和洛維工程公司的客戶。

湯姆： 我不肯定這是個好主意。

黛安： 湯姆，我認為這真是個好主意。讓凱倫盡快約見我們的客戶是很重要的。

湯姆： 當然，只是我在星期一晚留在樸茨茅斯，直到星期二晚才會駕車回倫敦。

凱倫： 湯姆，不要緊，我可以星期二早上坐火車回去。

約翰： 太好了，我想這是個好的解決方法。現在，我另外還有一個會議，恐怕……

黛安： 我也是。約翰，很高興能和你說話……凱倫。

凱倫： 好極了，很快和你們再談。黛安和羅拔，很高興和你們說話。湯姆，星期一見。

湯姆： 好的，那星期一再見。凱倫，很期待能見到你。

Translation of conversations

11 Making plans by email 通過電郵商定計劃

湯姆：

因應我們今天中午的電話會議，我有一個主意。<u>何不</u>星期一早<u>上我</u>和你一起去洛維銷售團隊的會議？

如果這樣可以的話，我們可以同時向銷售團隊的人展示 APU 公司的顧客關係管理分析工具。我們必須確保他們樂意使用這個工具。接着，<u>或者我們可以</u>所有人一起吃午飯，再在下午駕車到樸茨茅斯。<u>你對這個安排覺得怎樣？</u>

此外，我打算在樸茨茅斯的會議之後，在星期一晚上坐火車回倫敦。我和洛維法律部門的彼得・金約了星期二早上見面，所以我不能遲到。約翰也請我盡快檢查倫敦的系統，但我在星期五飛回悉尼之前沒有其他工作安排，所以<u>我們星期三早上再開會好嗎？</u>如果你方便的話，<u>能不能</u>在辦公室預訂一間會議室給我們？

祝 一切安好

凱倫

12 Telephone small talk 電話閒談

湯姆： 湯姆・菲特。

約翰： 湯姆，你好。我是約翰。

湯姆： 早晨…… 抱歉，午安，約翰。你那邊今天天氣怎樣？

約翰： 今天天氣很熱，電台説明天更熱！我兒子想我在週末帶他們到海灘，那他們可以去滑浪，而且我們可以一起燒烤。

湯姆： <u>聽起來真好！</u>倫敦這邊<u>正在下雨</u>。

約翰： 噢，<u>太可惜了！</u>你有沒有看昨晚的足球比賽？

湯姆： 沒有，我錯過了。

約翰： 那是一場精彩的球賽。<u>現在的工作怎樣？</u>

湯姆： 很困難！不是所有團隊都樂意見到這次合併，和我認為法律部門會更困難，但凱倫很快會和法律部主管彼得・金商談。

約翰： 對。嗯……湯姆，<u>我在想你可不可以</u>來我們悉尼的辦公室一趟？你可以在這邊留一個星期和見見這邊的人。

湯姆： 呃……好的，但你和黛安説過了嗎？

約翰： 還沒，她現在不在辦公室裏，我會晚一點再打給她。

湯姆： 我明白了。

約翰： 那麼，<u>甚麼時間對你方便</u>？

湯姆： 嗯，我要先查一下我的日程表，我會發電郵提出一些建議。這樣可以嗎？

約翰： 沒問題，我要和黛安談談。好，那你這個週末有甚麼事情要做？你會做……？

13 Arranging the business trip　安排出差

約翰：

　因應今早我們的電話交談，我看過我的日程表，十月二十日（星期一）開始的那個星期，是我來 APU 位於悉尼辦公室的好時間。

　如果你滿意安排，我就在那週前一個星期五從倫敦飛過來。請問 APU 可否幫我預訂在十月十七至二十四日的酒店房間？我將於十月二十五日飛回倫敦。

　有關我們討論的議程，我可以安排我們和黛安三人的電話會議，列出要討論的重要議題。如果你想的話，我也可以邀請其他人，例如會計部的羅拔•海頓和法律部門的彼得•金。請讓我知道你的想法。

祝　一切安好

湯姆

湯姆：

　謝謝你的電郵。可以，日期沒有問題，我們也期待能和你見面。我認為和黛安先在電話會議裏確認討論議程是個好主意，但我認為暫時不需要邀請羅拔和彼得。電話會議之後，凱倫會召開幾個會議，並邀請相關的人出席。

　我的助理皮雅•萊文會幫你安排住宿，她很快會發電郵給你。此外，你想在星期六傍晚做些甚麼嗎？可能是在船上吃晚飯？請讓我知道你是否滿意那樣的安排。

祝 一切順心

約翰

14 Priorities for the business trip　出差行程的先後緩急

預設錄音： 另一位參加者正在進入通話。

湯姆： 這是湯姆•菲特。

Translation of conversations

凱倫：湯姆，你好。我已經來了，約翰馬上就會來。你好嗎？

湯姆：噢，我很好。凱倫，你呢？

凱倫：好極了，謝謝。我很期待……

預設錄音：另外兩位參加者正在進入通話。

約翰：凱倫你好，湯姆和黛安，你們好，我是約翰。

黛安：我是黛安，大家好。

湯姆：好的，那麼我們開始吧。我們需要做一個議程，下星期讓我和悉尼 APU 那邊的人討論。

凱倫：首先，我想讓你看資料中心，那非常重要。

湯姆：是的，我同意。我想這個資料中心比倫敦的更大。

約翰：沒錯，然後你要和佛朗卡•梅商談，她是資料安全部的經理。

湯姆：好。

凱倫：之後，你一定要與我的團隊見面。他們可以告訴你未來五年我們電腦系統的發展計劃，這令人十分雀躍。

湯姆：我很肯定。接着我可以知道我們應為倫敦的系統做些甚麼。

凱倫：最後，我們要決定甚麼時候將洛維的會計系統轉為 APU 的系統。我們不可以再等太久，這件事十分重要。

黛安：湯姆，那麼看來你將會很忙！

15 Dealing with questions in the conference call 處理電話會議的提問

黛安：我同意湯姆的議程，但約翰，我認為我們應籌辦一個洛維和 APU 的高級管理層會議。我認為這對我們幫助真的很大。

約翰：嗯…… 為何你覺得現時這樣做是重要的？

黛安：我認為各部門的經理應聚首一堂，令大家可以明白洛維這些變動為何如此重要。

約翰：是的，但我不明白為何 APU 的經理也要參加，這樣開支會很大。

黛安：嗯……看來有些事情明顯不像預期中順利。

約翰：抱歉，但你可以重複一次嗎？我恐怕我聽不清楚你之前説甚麼。

黛安：噢，對不起。我認為如果這裏的人可與 APU 的管理人員見面，大家能合作得更好。

湯姆：而且我們可以解決一些誤解。

凱倫：你説的 "誤解" 是甚麼意思？

湯姆：我認為我們應該改善彼此的溝通。

約翰：原來如此，你可以給些例子嗎？

黛安：有些洛維的經理很難明白這些改變為何是必要的。例如會計系統，我們不應等到這裏的人發生問題。

約翰： 嗯，是的。黛安，按情況那可能是個好主意。我認為你和我應該寄邀請信給重要人物。你認為甚麼時候是理想的日期，還有應該在甚麼地方舉行會議呢？

16 Written invitations 撰寫邀請

主旨：請預留時間

各位同事：

　我們很高興邀請各位出席澳洲電力公司和洛維工程公司第一個高層管理人員聯合會議，本次活動將於倫敦一月十日舉行。

　本次活動會是一個機會，讓各位可與新同事見面和建立網絡。如各位能於十一月四日星期三前回覆電郵，答覆是否出席，不勝感激。

　當收到各位的回覆後，我們將會給各位發更多資料，包括一個詳盡的議程、講者名單、計劃的活動和酒店預約表格。

　我們很期待能在不久的將來歡迎各位來到倫敦。

你衷心的，
黛安・甘迺迪和約翰・卡特謹啟

黛安和約翰：

　很高興收到你們會議的邀請信，我認為這是一個很好的主意。我原本打算在那個星期去我們那邊巴西的辦事處，但我會盡量改動時間。當我知道我可以更改行程的時候，我會回覆你們確認我會出席。

祝 一切順心
維・桑達

17 Business trip details 出差詳情

菲特先生：

讓我來介紹自己 — 本人是卡特先生的行政助理，我想和閣下確認你的酒店安排。

我替你預訂了南方十字酒店七晚住宿（十月十七至二十四日）。酒店為閣下發了一個預訂的認證碼：TF18OCT24210。酒店有長轎車服務，如果閣下可以提供航班資料，本人會安排機場接送服務。有關酒店設施詳情，請查看酒店的網頁：
www.southern-cross.aus

卡特先生訂了悉尼歌劇院星期六傍晚《卡門》的歌劇門票，他六時半在酒店大堂等你。閣下可在下面找到歌劇團的劇評：
www.sydney_echo.com

本人期待能在十月二十日星期一歡迎閣下來到悉尼和 APU 的辦公室。如有任何疑問，請聯絡本人。

你摯誠的，
皮雅·萊文謹啟

18 Changes to the schedule 更改日程

皮雅： 皮雅·萊文，請問有甚麼可以幫你？

湯姆： 皮雅，你好。這是倫敦洛維工程公司的湯姆·菲特。

皮雅： 湯姆，你好。我有甚麼可以幫你做？

湯姆： 首先，很感謝你幫我預訂酒店。

皮雅： 我樂意效勞。

湯姆： 我想請你幫一個忙，請問我可以稍微改動一下日程嗎？

皮雅： 當然可以。

湯姆： 麻煩你幫我更改酒店的預訂，讓我十月十六日就到達嗎？

皮雅： 沒有問題。

湯姆： 而且我想問，你可否幫我安排在十九日星期天租一輛車？我想探望住在海邊的一些朋友，一輛小汽車就可以了。

皮雅： 當然。此外，湯姆，你之前有來過悉尼嗎？

湯姆： 不，我沒有。

皮雅： 請問你想我確定租車公司向你提供一輛有衛星定位的車嗎？那你就不會迷路了。

湯姆： 這是個好主意，非常感謝你一切的安排，皮雅。

皮雅： 別客氣。

湯姆： 還有你介不介意把詳情再電郵給我？那真要感謝你。

皮雅： 當然不介意。

19 Welcome back to the office 歡迎回到公司

黛安： 啊，湯姆！再見到你真好！

湯姆： 你好，黛安。回來真好。

黛安： 航班順利嗎？

湯姆： 噢，糟透了！我們因為技術問題要在很冷的莫斯科降落，我們在那裏逗留了六個小時。

黛安： 噢，天啊。你回來真好。你覺得和 APU 有關的一切都進行順利嗎？你星期五有沒有收到我的電郵？

湯姆： 有關 APU 和洛維的聯合管理層會議？對，我收到了，我認為 APU 的人對這個提議很感興趣。我可以在之後的項目會議提供更多細節給你。

黛安： 好極了。那麼你在悉尼怎樣？我記得那邊有些很好的意大利餐廳。

湯姆： 對！但那邊最好的餐廳是日式壽司店。

黛安： 你有去觀光嗎？

湯姆： 有，去了一些地方。約翰和他妻子帶了我去悉尼歌劇院去看《卡門》。

黛安： 你真幸運！

湯姆： 是的，那是個很不錯的傍晚。我的酒店房間可以眺望悉尼港口。那是最迷人的地方。

黛安： 那邊的天氣怎樣？

湯姆： 好極了！陽光充沛和非常炎熱，最熱的那天是三十五度。倫敦這邊下過雨，是嗎？

黛安： 是的，上星期每天都在下雨。

20 The project review 檢討項目

黛安： 那麼，湯姆，你是説約翰和凱倫不滿意項目的進度嗎？

湯姆： 是的，他們説我們進度太慢。

黛安： 那讓我們看看項目計劃吧。

湯姆： 好，這裏我們可以看到所有主要資訊科技的主題：人事資源系統的整合、會計和簿記的整合及銷售數據的整合。

黛安： 你可以讓我看看項目的進展狀態嗎？

湯姆： 下一幅圖表顯示人力資源系統詳細的日程表：工資總額、社會保障福利、表現評價和培訓紀錄，全部已和 APU 的系統整合了。

黛安： 太好了！你開始培訓人力資源部職員使用新系統的課程了嗎？

湯姆： 哦，我們已經完成那個課程，我們在上個月完成的。

黛安： 好的，那麼你會在甚麼時候完成其他所有工作？

湯姆： 接下來，會計系統的整合工作，恐怕進度落後了，我們還沒將資料轉移到 APU。

黛安： 噢，你可否解釋一下為甚麼還沒有轉移？

湯姆： APU 搜集資料的方法和我們不同，這是一個問題。

黛安： 但我不明白為甚麼這會是個問題，資料是相同的，只是放在不同地方。

湯姆： 最大問題是羅拔的會計團隊太小，不能完成所有工作，但我已告訴他們，要在一月尾之前完成。

黛安： 真的嗎？你何時做的？

湯姆： 我上星期在悉尼時和他們開了一個電話會議。

黛安： 我明白，那很好。

湯姆： 繼續下去？

黛安： 當然。

21 Starting the video conference 開始視像會議

黛安： 所以我只要輸入號碼⋯⋯像這樣⋯⋯然後我們應該可以見到約翰和凱倫。他們在那裏，這個視像會議的設備好極了！你好，約翰，你好，凱倫，你們能聽到我們的聲音嗎？對不起，你的聲音從器材傳送過來似乎運作不正常。

凱倫： ⋯⋯然後如果我們按這個掣，我們應該能夠聽到他們的聲音。啊！是黛安！你能夠聽到我們的聲音嗎？

黛安： 那好多了。

凱倫： 請等一等，現在的影像好像有些問題。

凱倫： 黛安，湯姆？我們的影像好像有問題，你能見到我們嗎？

湯姆： 見到，而且我們能夠聽到你們的聲音！

約翰： 我想我們的系統壞了！我們看不到任何東西！

凱倫： 啊，我不明白。當我按開始按掣時，甚麼反應也沒有。

約翰： 黛安，抱歉讓你們等了這麼長時間。凱倫弄不好這部器材，而我也不懂怎樣做。

凱倫： 我想我要打電話給技術人員。請等一下！

黛安： 別擔心，我完全明白，我們可以等。

22 Discussing problems in the video conference 在視像會議上討論問題

約翰： 啊，太好了！我們現在可以看到和聽到你們了。東尼，謝謝你。

黛安： 好極了！那麼我想我們需要討論項目進度。

凱倫： 對。人力資源和銷售部的整合工作很順利，只是你們的會計師是個問題。他們似乎不想用我們的會計系統，所以他們做每件事的速度都很慢。

黛安： 凱倫，我不同意。我們的會計師要仔細檢查你們的系統以確保⋯⋯

凱倫： 是的，但現在已過了三個月！我認為你應對羅拔•海頓的團隊施加更多壓力。

湯姆： 我不確定那樣做會否有用。他們現在工作太多，人手卻不足夠，他們需要幫助。

黛安： 我也是這樣想。他們需要更多資源，而不是壓力。

約翰： 也許我應和羅拔談談，解釋這事為何這樣重要。

黛安： 你看，我很抱歉，但我不認為這是個好主意。羅拔很清楚這為甚麼很重要，我們只需要給他多一點時間。

凱倫： 我恐怕那不可能。我們要在一月的新財政年度之前完成系統整合。

約翰： 對，我同意。你沒辦法在沒有財政資料的情況下經營。

黛安： 你說的完全對，所以我們要看能否找到另一個方法解決這個問題。

23 Finding solutions in the video conference 在視像會議上尋求解決方法

黛安： 所以，這是現在的情況：你想洛維會計部的資訊科技系統和 APU 的整合起來。但我們沒有足夠人手很快完成它，而且如果在新的財政年度之前，還沒有完成的話，我們就會有麻煩。所以，我們可以怎樣做？

凱倫： 僱用額外的資訊科技人員怎樣？

約翰： 我不認為那是可行的方法。

湯姆： 約翰，我同意你的觀點。資訊科技人員可能很昂貴，而且無論如何，他們不熟悉我們兩家公司。

黛安： 這也是我的想法，解釋每件事花太長時間。但你們派些會計師過來幫助羅拔的團隊又如何？

湯姆： 好主意，也派些資訊科技的專家過來好不好？

約翰： 如果那是必要的話，我們總是可以看看有沒有一些資訊科技人員可以幫忙。

凱倫： 但首先，你們何不與羅拔確認一下，在新系統裏他需要甚麼幫忙？

約翰： 凱倫，好主意。湯姆，你可否發些資料過來，讓我們看看問題在哪裏？

湯姆： 我今天馬上做。

黛安： 好極了。約翰，如果我們告訴你我們需要甚麼人，你會盡快派你們的人來嗎？

約翰： 我們盡力而為，這是很重要的事。

24 Ending the video conference 結束視像會議

約翰： 所以，我們今天的討論包括每件事了嗎？

黛安： 是的，我想已包括了一切。

約翰： <u>所以，重溫一次</u>。我打算告訴會計部的主管，他們的一些專家要飛住倫敦幾個星期。

凱倫： 然後，我也會檢查哪些資訊科技的專家可派來你們這邊。

黛安： 好極了！有了這個解決方法，我真的覺得會計系統能夠如期整合。

約翰： 太好了！有人可以為我們的團隊安排酒店住宿和保安通行證嗎？

黛安： 沒問題。我的個人助理茉莉可以處理那些。

約翰： 啊，對，茉莉！那麼，<u>我們下次應何時見面</u>？

湯姆： 甚麼時間對你最方便？

約翰： 好，<u>讓我查一下日程表</u>。啊，下星期四同樣時間，你可以嗎？

黛安： 那<u>我沒問題</u>。

湯姆： 我也是。

凱倫： 還有我！

湯姆： 我應該寄邀請信和安排視像會議嗎？

約翰： 啊，是的，湯姆，謝謝你，那很好。所以，我們很快再聯繫。黛安，下星期我們必須討論高級管理層的會議。

黛安： 這個主意非常好。我很期待，那麼再見！

湯姆： <u>下星期見了</u>。

凱倫： 再見。

約翰： 保重！

Key phrases for speaking

Greeting colleagues 問候同事

Good morning / Morning! / Good afternoon. / Afternoon! 早晨！
Hi! 你好！
Hello, ... How are you? 你好，……你好嗎？
Fine thanks, and you? 我很好，謝謝，你呢？
Very well! 非常好！

Talking about your weekend 談論你的週末

Good weekend? 週末過得好嗎？
Great, thanks! 好極了，謝謝！
How was your weekend? 你的週末過得如何？
Very busy! 非常忙！

Making small talk 閒聊

Good to see you again. 再見到你真好。
It's good / nice to be back. 回來真好。
Well, it's good / nice to have you back. 嗯，你回來真好。

Asking about and describing past experiences 談過去的經驗

Good flight? / How was the flight? 航班一切順利嗎？/航班怎樣？
What did you get up to / do? 你會做甚麼事？
Did you do any sightseeing? 你有沒有去觀光？
What was the weather like? 天氣怎樣？
Lucky you! 你真幸運！
It was awful! 太可怕了！
Great! 好極了！

Welcoming company guests and exchanging business cards
歡迎公司訪客和交換名片

Good to see you again! 很高興再見到你！
Good to see you again too. 我也很高興再見到你。
Can I introduce you to ...? 讓我向你介紹……？
Nice to meet you. 很高興認識你。
Nice to meet you too. 我也很高興認識你。
Please, call me XYZ. 請叫我……
Let me introduce .... 讓我來介紹……
Pleased to meet you both. 很高興能認識你們。
Pleased to meet you too. 我也很高興認識你。
Let me give you my card. 讓我給你我的名片。
Here's my card. 這是我的名片。
What do you do? 你是做甚麼的？

Offering refreshments to guests 向客人提供茶點

Help yourself to something. 隨便吃點甚麼。
Could you pass me ...? 你可否把……遞給我？
Sorry, is that chicken? 對不起，那是雞肉嗎？
I'm afraid I don't eat meat. 我恐怕我不能吃肉。
Would you like some ...? 你想要些……嗎？
Have some .... 要些……。
It's delicious. 很好吃。

Starting meetings and making requests 開始會議和提出請求

Thank you for coming to this meeting. 謝謝各位來到這個會議。
Let's start by +ing .... 首先……。
I want you to .... 我想你……。
I would / I'd like you to .... 我希望你……
We really need you to .... 我們真的很需要你……。
Could you ...? 你可以……？
Would you mind if I ...? 你介意我……嗎？

Checking progress 檢查進展

Is everything going well with ...? 和……一切進展良好嗎？
Is everything OK with ...? 和……一切順利嗎？

Using slides in a meeting / presentation 開會或演示時用投影片

Let's look at .... 讓我們看……。
Here we can see .... 這裏我們可以看……。
The next slide shows .... 下一張投影片展示……。
Moving on to .... 到下一張……。

Asking questions in a meeting 開會時提問題

Can you show me ...? 你可否把……給我看？
Have you ... yet? 你已做……了嗎？
When will you finish ...? 你甚麼時候完成……？
Can you explain why ...? 你可否解釋為何……？
I don't understand why .... 我不明白為何……
When did you (do) that? 你何時做那事？
Can you tell me ...? 你能否告訴我……？
Why do you have ...? 你為何會有……？
How much ...? 多少……？
How many ...? 多少……？

Agreeing 同意
That's right. 那是對的。
Yes, I agree. 是，我同意。
I think so too. 我也是這樣想。
You're absolutely right. 你完全正確。

Disagreeing 不同意

I don't agree. 我不同意。
Yes, but …. 是，但是……
I'm not sure that's going to work. 我不肯定那是否可行。
I'm sorry but I don't think that's a good idea. 對不起，但我不認為那是個好主意。
I'm afraid that's not possible. 我恐怕那沒有可能。

Summarizing the situation 總結情況

So, this is the situation: …. 所以，這情況是：……。
So, to sum up: …. 所以，總結是：……。

Making proposals 提出建議

What about -ing …? …… 怎樣？
How about -ing …? …… 如何？
What if you / we …? 如果你或我們…… 怎樣？
Why don't you/we …? 你或我們何不……？

Discussing possibilities 討論可能性

What can we do? 我們能做甚麼？
We could always …. 我們總是能夠……。
We can do this or we can do that. 我們可以做這事或我們可以做那事。

Ending a meeting 結束會議

Have we covered everything today? 我們今天要談的事都談過了嗎？
I think that covers everything. 我想那包含一切。
Are you OK with that? 你滿意那樣的安排嗎？
So to recap, …. 所以，要扼要簡述，……。
Let me summarize: …. 讓我總結一下：……。
I think that's enough for today. 我想今天就到此為止吧。

Arranging a new appointment 安排見面

When should we next meet? 我們下次該何時見面？
When is a good time for you? 哪個時間對你方便？
Let me check my schedule. 讓我查一下時間表。
Does XYZ suit you? …… 適合你嗎？
That's good for me! 那最合我心意！
See you next week then. 下星期見你。

Starting a presentation 開始匯報

I would like / I'd like to tell you something about …. 我會跟你説有關……
First, …. / First of all, …. 第一，…… / 首先，……
Second, …. 第二，……
Third, …. 第三，……
Next …, 其次……，
Finally, …. 最後，……

Questions and answers at a presentation 匯報中的問答

Do you have any questions? 你有沒有問題？
Sorry, I don't understand your question. 抱歉，我不明白你的問題。
I'm glad you asked that question. 很高興你問那條問題。
That's a good question. 那是一條好問題。
I'm not sure about that. 我不太肯定那事。
(Now) I have a question for you, Tom. 湯姆，我有條問題想問你。
Let me think. 讓我想想。

Talking about the past 談及過去的事

After ..., we did .... 在……之後，我們做……。
Then .... 然後……。

Calling a business partner 打電話給生意伙伴

Hello, this is Tom Field from .... 你好，我是……的湯姆・菲特。
Can I speak to Karen Taylor, please? 請問我可以和凱倫・泰萊說話嗎？
Can you put me through to ...? 你可以幫我接駁給……嗎？
I'll call back later. 我之後會再打電話來。
I'll send her an email. 我會發電郵給她。
Thanks for your help. 謝謝你的幫忙。

Answering the phone 接聽電話

Kim Benders speaking. / This is Kim Benders speaking. / Kim Benders. 這是金・本德。
I'm afraid she's not in the office. 抱歉她不在辦公室。
She's on a business trip to .... 她到……出差。
Can I help you? 請問我有甚麼可以幫你？
Hold the line, please. / Can you (please) hold? 請稍等。
I'm sorry but his line's busy at the moment. 抱歉但他正在通電話。
Can I take a message? 我可否寫下留言？

Starting telephone conferences 開始電話會議

Tom here. 我是湯姆。
I'm sitting here with Karen. 我和凱倫坐在一起。
I'm calling from home. 我在家裏打電話過來。
I'm working at / from home today. 我今天在家裏工作。
Diane will call in in a minute. 黛安馬上打電話來。
Sorry we're late. 抱歉，我們遲到了。
Let's start. 讓我們開始吧。

Key phrases for speaking

Describing technical problems in telephone and video conferences 描述電話及錄像會議的技術問題

There seems to be something wrong with .... ……似乎出了某些差錯。
I'm having trouble with .... 我……遇到了麻煩。
I think my XYZ has crashed. 我想我的……壞了。
The XYZ doesn't seem to be working. ……似乎不能正常操作。
When I click on the XYZ, nothing happens. 我點一下……，甚麼也沒發生。
I think I need to call a technician. 我想我需要找技術員。

Dealing with delays 處理延誤

Just a moment. 稍等片刻。
Hold on a minute. 稍等一下。
Sorry to keep you waiting. 抱歉讓你等了那麼久。

Telephone small talk 電話閒聊

How's the weather ...? …… 天氣怎樣？
How's work at the moment? / What's work like at the moment? 工作現在怎樣？/ 現在工作看來怎樣？
Did you see the football / basketball game last night? 昨晚你看足球 / 籃球比賽了嗎？
What are you doing this weekend? 這個週末你會做甚麼？
What are your plans for this weekend? 這個週末你計劃做甚麼？
It's raining here. 這裏正在下雨。
Sounds great. 看來好極了。
Too bad. 太糟糕。

Making suggestions and arrangements 建議及安排

I was wondering if you could .... 我想你是否可以……。
When is a good time for you? 甚麼時間對你最方便？
I have to check my schedule. 我要檢查我的時間表。

Making arrangements 安排

I just want to let you know .... 我只想讓你知道……。
What are your plans on ...? 你對……有甚麼計劃？
Let me check my schedule for next week. 讓我查一查我下星期的時間表。
How does Monday afternoon look? 下星期一下午怎樣？
Let me take a look. 讓我看一下。

Prioritizing 先後次序

First of all .... / First .... / Firstly .... 首先……
Next.... 之後……
Second / Secondly .... 第二……
After that, ... 在那之後，……
Third / Thirdly .... 第三……
Finally .... 最後……
That's very important / crucial. 那非常重要 / 至關重要。

Asking for repetition 請求重複

I'm sorry but could you repeat that? 我很抱歉但你可否重複那部份？
I'm afraid / sorry I didn't hear what you said. 我恐怕 / 抱歉我聽不到你剛才説甚麼。

Asking for explanations 請求解釋

Is there a reason why ...? 是否有原因可解釋……？
Yes, but I don't understand why .... 對，但我不明白為何……。
What do you mean by ...? 你説……是甚麼意思？
Can you give an example? 你可否給一個例子？

Offering help 提供協助

How can I help you? 我可以怎樣幫你？
What can I do for you? 我可以為你做點甚麼？
Would you like me to ...? 你想我……？

Making a request 邀請

I wonder if I can ask you for a favour? 我想我是否可以請你幫一個忙？
Could you do me a favour? 你可否幫我一個忙？
Please could I / you change ...? 我 / 你可否改……？
I wanted to ask if you could .... 我想問你可否……。
Would you mind sending me an email? 你可否發電郵給我？

Giving thanks 感謝

Thanks very much for ... +*ing* .... 感謝……。
Thanks a lot for your help with the arrangements. 感謝你幫忙安排。
That would be really kind. 那樣真好。

Saying goodbye 説再見

Good to speak to you, ... 能和你談很好，……。
Speak to you soon. 很快和你談。
Nice speaking to you, ... 能和你談很不錯，……。
I'm looking forward to it. 我很期待它。

Key phrases for writing

Business emails 商業電郵

I tried to call / phone you ... but .... 我嘗試打電話給你…… / 但是……。
With regard to ... , 有關……,
I look forward to speaking to you soon. 我期待很快可以和你談。

Best wishes 祝一切順心。

Making suggestions and appointments 提出建議和安排

I think it's a good idea if .... 我認為……是一個好主意。
I suggest that I .... 我提議我……。
Could you let me know if that's convenient for you? 請問你可否讓我知道那對你方便嗎？

Emailing to make arrangements 用電郵安排預約

Following our phone call, ... 因應今早的電話……。
Thanks for your email. 謝謝你的電郵。
The week starting / ending .... ……那週開始 / 結束。

Regarding .... / As regards .... 關於…… / 有關……。

Please let me know. 請讓我知道你的想法。
Let me know if that's .... 請讓我知道你是否……

Best regards / wishes, ... 祝一切安好 / 順心，……

Automated replied 自動回覆

I am out of the office [in ...] until .... 我在……之前不在辦公室。

Making suggestions 建議

Why don't I ...? 我何不……？
If this is OK for you, ... 如果你滿意這樣的安排，……。
Perhaps we could .... 也許我們可以……

Requests and asking for opinions 邀請及詢問意見

How do you feel about this? / What's your opinion about ...? 你覺得怎樣？ / 你對……有甚麼意見？
Shall we ...? 我們……好嗎？
Do you think you could ...? / Would you mind +ing ...? 你能否…… ？ / 你介不介意…… ？

Asking for support / help 尋求支持 / 幫助

Would it be possible for ... to ...? ……是否可能…… ？

Looking after visitors 照顧訪客

Let me introduce myself – I'm .... 讓我介紹自己 —— 我是⋯⋯。

I would like to confirm .... 我想確認⋯⋯。
I will arrange for.... 我將安排⋯⋯。
For detailed information about .... 關於⋯⋯的詳細資料。
Please check .... 請查⋯⋯。
You can find .... 你可以找到⋯⋯。
Please contact me if you have any questions. 如果你有任何問題請聯繫我。

Formal email invitations 正式電郵邀請

Dear Colleagues

We are pleased to invite you to ....
The event will take place on ....
This occasion will be an opportunity to network with ....
We would be grateful if you ....
We look forward to welcoming you to ....
... in the near future

Yours truly

致全體同事

我們很高興邀請你⋯⋯。
該活動會在⋯⋯舉行。
這場合將會是與⋯⋯聯絡的機會。
如果你能⋯⋯，我們深表謝意。
我們期望歡迎你⋯⋯。
⋯⋯在不久的將來。

你摯誠的

Key words

Companies

	Your translation
boss	
branch	
colleague / co-worker	
department	
division	
employee	
employer	
headquarters	
job	
to manage	

Departments

	Your translation
Accounting	
Customer Services	
Distribution	
Human Resources [HR]	
Information Technology (IT)	
Logistics	
Marketing	
Payroll	
Production	
Research and Development	
Sales	
Security	
Transport [UK] / Transportation [US]	
Warehousing	

Events and meetings	
	Your translation
agenda	
agreement	
boardroom	
catering	
change	
compromise	
conference room	
equipment	
event	
facilities	
flip chart	
invitation	
meeting room	
negotiation	
participant	
presentation	
projector	
time out	
to agree	
to argue	
to arrange	
to attend	
to book	
to bring forward	
to cancel	
to disagree	
to make a deal	
to invite	
to negotiate	
to organize	
to put / move back	
to reserve	

Key words

In the office

	Your translation
chair	
computer	
cubicle / work station	
desk	
fax machine	
hole punch (UK) / hole puncher (US)	
paper	
paper clip	
pen	
pencil	
photocopy / copy	
printout	
stapler	
stationery	
telephone / phone	
to email	
to fax	
to forward	
to print something [out]	
to staple	

Emails

	Your translation
disclaimer	
greeting	
out-of-office notice	
recipient	
sender	
subject	
to CC	
to contact	
to delete	
to email	
to forward	

Office job titles

	Your translation
administrative assistant	
chairman / chairwoman / chair / chair person	
chief executive officer [CEO]	
chief financial officer [CFO]	
Chief operating officer [COO]	
clerk	
consultant	
engineer	
lawyer	
manager	
managing director	
personal assistant	
receptionist	
salesman / saleswoman / salesperson / sales rep [representative]	
secretary	

Telephoning

	Your translation
busy (line)	
cell (US) / mobile (UK) phone	
engaged (line) (UK)	
extension	
line	
mobile (UK) phone / cell phone (US)	
to call (US)	
to call back	
to connect *someone to someone*	
to hold (*the line*)	
to put *someone* through *to someone*	

Key words

Travel	
	Your translation
flight	
car hire (UK) / car rental (US)	
journey	
plane	
subway (US) / underground (UK)	
taxi	
tour	
traffic	
train	
trip	

Presentations	
	Your translation
audience	
conclusion	
handout	
laser pointer	
multimedia projector	
overview	
slide	
screen	
to make a presentation	
to present	
to sum up	

Projects	Your translation
Act of God	
budget	
clause	
client	
contract	
cost	
customer	
deadline	
delay	
delivery	
goal	
kick-off meeting	
main contractor	
penalty	
phase	
plan	
progress	
project	
project leader / manager / member / team	
project meeting	
project room	
quality	
resources	
schedule	
status	
strike	
subcontractor	
supplier	
time	
timeline	

Present continuous 現在進行式

肯定形式：

- I'm [I am] **waiting** for my taxi.
- We're [We are] **staying** at the Anchor Hotel.
- They're [They are] **having** a meeting.

否定形式：

- No, I'm **not staying** in the country.
- She **isn't** [She is not] waiting for Diane.

提問：

- **Are** you **staying** at the Anchor Hotel?
- **Is** Mr Jones **waiting** to see me?
- When are they **leaving**?

長答案：

- Yes. I'm **staying** at the Anchor.
- No, I'm **not staying** in London.

短答案：

- Yes, I **am**.
- Yes, she **is**.
- Yes, they **are**.
- No, I'm **not**.
- No, she **isn't**.
- No, they **aren't**.

這時態用作描述正在進行的動作：

- Would you like an umbrella because it's **raining** (now)?

或一個尚未完成的動作：

- I'm **waiting** to see him.

它可用以描述短暫的動作或情況：

- She's **staying** at the Anchor Hotel in London for three nights.

常用於現在進行式的詞語有：now, at the moment, presently

Future meaning 含將來意思

現在進行式用於討論已計劃和安排但未發生的活動。

- I**'m staying** in the hotel next week too.
- We**'re playing** golf with Yoshi on Saturday.
- He**'s meeting** them on Monday.
- He**'s** not **flying** to New York until after Friday the 13th.
- **Are** you **giving** a talk at the data security conference next month?
- **Is** he **coming** to Germany soon?

使用這種形式可用作解釋或借口，因為我們知道計劃已確定。

- Sorry, I can't come on Monday. **I'm driving** to Frankfurt.

注意 — 以下動詞不常用於現在進行式
remember, understand, want, like, belong, suppose, need, seem, prefer, believe, know, think (= believe), hear, smell, have (= possess).

Exercise 1

將括號內的動詞轉為現在式或現在進行式以完成句子。

Tom Field and Diane Kennedy both 1) _____ (work) for Lowis Engineering. At the moment Diane 2) _____ (focus) on the integration of Lowis Engineering into APU and Tom 3) _____(help) her. Tom usually 4) _____ (arrive) at work at about 8.30 am, but today he 5) _____ (stay) at home because he 6) _____(not feel) well.

Exercise 2

重組句子。

1 APU / is / next / visiting / the / Diane / offices / month.
2 going / Aren't / to / the / you / Saturday / party / on?
3 afraid / we're / I'm / visiting / mother / this / my / weekend.
4 isn't / Tuesday / arriving / She / until.
5 o'clock / meeting / at / They're / the / President / three.
6 he / flying / Is / soon / to / LA?

Present simple 一般現在式

肯定形式：

- I **work** at the reception desk.
- She **enjoys** her job very much.
- Our employees **love** helping visitors.

否定形式：

- I **don't [do not] work** for Lowis Engineering.
- This visitor **doesn't [does not]** have a security card.
- We **don't allow** pets in the company.

提問：

- **Does** she **work** for Lowis Engineering?
- Where **do** you **come** from?

長答案：

- Yes, she **does work** for Lowis Engineering.
- No, she **doesn't work** for Lowis Engineering.

短答案：

- Yes, I **do**.
- No, I **don't**.
- Yes, she **does**.
- **No, she doesn't.**

這種時態是用於表達事實：

- Tom **works** at Lowis Engineering in London but he **lives** in Croydon.
- The office **is** on the corner of Wardour Street and Oxford Street.
- Diane **works** in London but she comes from the USA.

也用於定期或例行活動：

- I **check** my emails every day.
- The mailman **brings** the mail before lunch.

也用於表達時間表和日程：

- The cafeteria **opens** at 12 o'clock.
- The company **closes** at midnight.

常用於一般現在式的詞語包括：often, seldom, usually, never, always, normally, rarely：

- It **often rains** a lot in April.
- We **never close**.

Exercise 3

將括號內的動詞轉為現在式來完成問句和答案。

1 Where _____ you _____ from? (come)
2 I _____ from Venice. (come)
3 Who _____ you _____ for? (work)

4　I _____ for an electronics company. (work)
5　What time _____ your boss _____ in the office? (arrive)
6　She usually _____ to the office at about eight o'clock. (get)
7　How often _____ she _____ on vacation? (go)
8　She never _____ any vacation at all! (take)

Going to future　將來式

肯定形式：

- **I'm [I am] going to** send an email tomorrow.
- They**'re [They are] going to** complain about the meeting.
- He**'s [He is] going to** book three conference rooms.
- We**'re going to** write to the manager.

否定形式：

- **I'm not** [I **am not**] **going to** telephone tomorrow.
- We **aren't** [We **are not**] **going to** eat in the restaurant tonight.
- She **isn't going to go to** Australia.

提問：

- **Are you going to** telephone tomorrow?
- **Is he going to** tell the boss?
- Who**'s going to** tell the boss?

長答案：

- Yes, I**'m going to** telephone tomorrow.
- No, **I'm not going to** telephone tomorrow.
- Yes, they**'re going to** email the manager.
- No, they **aren't going to** email the manager.

短答案：

- Yes, I **am**.
- No, I**'m not**.
- Yes, he **is**.
- No, he **isn't**.
- Yes, they **are**.
- No, they **aren't**.

這個時態用於說明一些已計劃或決定了，並且肯定會發生的事：

- We're **going to** move offices next year.
- When **are** you **going to** get a company car?
- When I get home, I'm **going to** write a report about the conference.

Exercise 4

使用框內詞語完成句子。

I'm	is	isn't	going	not	to

1 When I get to the office, _____ going to have a meeting with Robert.
2 Next summer we're _____ to spend some time sailing in the Mediterranean.
3 _____ he going to come to the conference?
4 John and Karen phoned. They aren't going _____ be here on time.
5 _____ Robert going to finish the integration by the end of December? I don't think so!

Past simple 一般過去式

肯定形式：

- He **arrived** yesterday.
- I **cancelled** my meeting last week.
- We **visited** the company last month.
- She **knew** there was a delay.
- We **ate** in the restaurant last night.

did 用於否定形式和提問形式：

- He **didn't [did not] telephone** yesterday.
- You **didn't tell** me that she was here.
- They **didn't enjoy** their visit.
- I **didn't expect** to wait so long at reception.
- **Did** Mr. Lawson **arrive** yesterday?
- **Did** you **enjoy** your visit?
- **Did** the suppliers **receive** their money?
- What **did** you **buy** in London?

長答案：

- Yes, he **arrived** yesterday.
- No, he **didn't arrive** yesterday.
- Yes, we **spoke** to the manager about your problem.
- No, we **didn't speak** to the manager about your problem.

短答案：

- Yes, we **did**.
- No, we **didn't**.
- Yes, I **did**.
- No, I **didn't**.

這個時態用於過去已完成的動作，可以是很久以前或最近發生的：

- I **visited** your company last week.
- Columbus **sailed** to America in 1492.

常用於一般過去式的詞語有：yesterday, an hour ago, last year, in 2009, last week, a year ago

Exercise 5

將括號內的詞語轉為正確的過去式形式（正面、負面、提問）來完成句子。

1 I _____ the report before I went home. (finish)
2 She _____ to me after the meeting. (not speak)
3 _____ Tom _____ Karen yesterday evening? (telephone)
4 What _____ Diane _____ about the problem? (do)
5 They _____ me the report on time. (not email)
6 I _____ a meeting last night with John. (have)

Simple future – will 一般將來式 — will

肯定形式：

- I**'ll** [I **will**] **mail** it tomorrow.
- We**'ll arrange** a meeting.
- Tom**'ll call me** as soon as your taxi is here.

否定形式：

- I **won't** [**will not**] **do** it tomorrow.
- John **won't forget** to do it, Karen.
- They **won't come** back.

提問：

- **Will** you **do** it tomorrow?
- **Will** she **call** me a taxi?
- When **will** my taxi **come**?

長答案：

- Yes, I'**ll do** it in a minute.
- No, **I won't do** it today.

短答案：

- Yes, **I will**.
- No, **I won't**.

這個時態用於預測將來：

- In the year 2020 we'**ll** all work until we are 75.
- You'**ll** never finish that report before 1:00.

它也用於有關未來的資料（不包括意向或安排）：

- In ten minutes we'**ll test** the fire alarm.

在條件句如 if- 句式時，必須使用它。

- If you **do not cancel** in time, you'll have to pay a fee.

它也用於宣佈對於提議的決定、承諾和威脅、請求和説明及建議：

- That sounds good. I'**ll have** the steak too.
- I'**ll tell** you as soon as the report is ready.
- I promise I'**ll inform** my boss immediately.
- Do that again and I'**ll complain** to your boss.
- **Will** you **fill in** this form, please?

Exercise 6

從不同的對話配對句子。

1	Can I speak to Catherine, please?	A	I'll find a new job!
2	You were fired! What'll you do now?	B	Don't worry, I'll send it again.
3	When can we have lunch?	C	Oh yes. I'll probably see them after lunch.
4	Will you see Tony and Andrea today?	D	You're right. I'll speak to the boss about the problem.
5	I can't find the report you emailed me.	E	Of course. I'll get her.
6	We don't have enough people!	F	Wait a moment and I'll check my calendar.

Phrasal verbs 短語動詞

- I must **call up** Robert.
- Can you **put** me **through to** John?
- **Hold on** and I'll (I will) connect you.

- Don't **put down** the receiver.
- John **picked up** the receiver when the phone rang.
- Can you **fill in** the form?
- 2,000 workers were **laid off** by the company.
- He **got up** at six o'clock in the morning.

短語動詞組合了動詞如 call、put、hold 和介詞如 down、up、through 等。許多短語動詞可以分拆成兩部份。

- Karen can **pick** Tom **up** from the airport.
- Kim **put** the cup of coffee **down** on the table.

以下是更多實用例子，記下你遇到的短語動詞，加它們入這個清單內。

- back up – make a copy of something
- set up – start a business
- close down – stop a business
- cut off – disconnect
- hold up – cause a delay
- turn on / off – start / stop a piece of electrical equipment

Prepositions of time 時間介詞

- The meeting is **at** ten o'clock.
- We close the office **at** Christmas time.
- I'm meeting Karen **at** lunchtime / the weekend [UK] / night.
- The next conference is **in** June.
- The company was founded **in** 1981.
- We need to organize a team-building exercise **in** the spring.
- China is going to be the most powerful economy **in** the 21st century.
- We had tea **in** the afternoon.
- I saw him **on** Wednesday.
- She sent me the email **on** Friday afternoon.
- I'm flying back to London **on** New Years Eve.
- The new offices were opened **on** Monday July 21st.
- I usually play tennis **on** the weekends. [US]

at、on 和 in 與這些時間介詞連用。

at – particular times, festival times and specific fixed expressions
in – months, years, seasons, centuries, parts of the day
on – days of the week, parts of named days, festival days, dates

Exercise 7

用 at、in 或 on 完成句子。

1　John and Karen are flying ＿＿＿＿＿＿ Sunday morning to London.
2　APU bought Lowis Engineering ＿＿＿＿＿＿ 2012.
3　We have a meeting with the lawyers ＿＿＿＿＿＿ 10.30.
4　APU plans to roll out the new software ＿＿＿＿＿＿ the summer.
5　I received the report ＿＿＿＿＿＿ Christmas day.
6　The workshops take place ＿＿＿＿＿＿ the weekend. [UK]

How much / many / a little / a few

- How **much time** do we have?
- Do you have **many offices** in Asia?
- I don't have **much coffee**.
- The company doesn't have **many servers**.
- He only has **a little money** in the bank.
- They have **a few people** in New York.
- There are only **a few salespeople**.

many 和 a few 用於可數名詞，例如 people、offices、chairs。much 和 a little 用於不可數名詞，例如 money、time、space、water、information、capacity。much 和 many 多用於問題及否定形式。

Exercise 8

在句子的正確詞語下面加底線。

1　He isn't paying *many / much* money for the information.
2　Britain doesn't have *much /many* mountains.
3　We only interviewed *a few / a little* colleagues about the problem.
4　How *much / many* factories does the company have in Ukraine?
5　There's only *a few / a little* water in the cooling system.
6　How *much / many* luggage does she have?

Modals for obligation 表示義務的情態動詞：must、have to、mustn't、don't have to

肯定形式：

- **I must speak** to my boss.
- **I have to fly** to Sydney.
- Karen **has to take** a taxi to the station.
- We **must have** a meeting about this.

情態動詞用於表示有義務或有必要做某事。

must 用於表示重大的個人義務或強而有力的個人勸告。

- I **must telephone** my mother this evening.

have to 用於表示因外在規則或情況而出現的義務。

- The bad weather means we **have to cancel** the picnic.

否定形式：

- You **mustn't (must not) speak** to him about this.
- She **doesn't (does not) have** to come to work tomorrow.
- I **mustn't (must not) forget** to book a hotel room.

must not 用於表示某事被禁止。

- You **mustn't (must not) smoke** in the office.

don't have to 用於表示某事並非必要。

- I **don't have to wear** a tie in the office.

問題形式：

- **Do** we **have to** send the report by Friday?
- **Does** he **have to check** the documents again?
- What **do** they **have to do** next?

長答案：

- Yes, we **have to**.
- No, we **don't have to send** it by then.

短答案：

- Yes, we **do**. / No, we **don't**.

Exercise 9

用 must、have to、mustn't 或 don't have to 完成句子。

1 Our accountant says we _____ pay our taxes this week.
2 We _____ go to lunch some time soon.
3 Why do we _____ take a plane? We can go by train.
4 If you want to drive home after the party, then you really _____ drink any alcohol.
5 The boss says we _____ meet him in his office in ten minutes.
6 I'm not feeling well. I _____ finish the report today, so I'm going home.

Comparison of adjectives 形容詞比較

比較級形容詞用來比較兩個事物。
一個音節的形容詞加-er
Rich → richer
以-y 結尾的形容詞變為 -ier
Lazy → lazier
含兩個或以上音節的形容詞在前面加 more / less
Difficult → more / less difficult
比較級多數用 than

- The Pacific is larger than the Atlantic

注意！

有些形容詞的比較級是不規則形式：
good → better
bad → worse
far → further / farther
big → bigger

Exercise 10

用括號內形容詞的比較級完成句子。

1 I don't like this job. It's _____ (hard) than I thought it would be.
2 Diane said the restaurant was _____ (good) than the cafeteria.
3 I want to take the train instead of flying because it's _____ (cheap).
4 I need some pills. My headache is much _____ (bad) now.
5 Everybody is _____ (happy) now that we've moved offices.
6 This project is _____ (difficult) than we expected.

Superlatives 最高級形式

最高級形式用於將一個類別或群組其中的一個成員與整類或全組作出比較。含一個音節的短形容詞，加 the 及 -est 構成最高級形式。

- Germany has **the largest economy** in Europe.

長形容詞會在其前面加 the most / the least。

- The Ritz is **the most expensive hotel** in London.

We decided to travel by bus. It was **the least expensive** option.

不規則形式：
有些常用形容詞的最高級是不規則形式：
good → the best
bad → the worst

far → the farthest / furthest
big → the biggest

Exercise 11

用括號內正確的形容詞最高級形式來完成句子。

1   London is _____ (big) city in the European Union.
2   My flight was delayed by 24 hours. It was _____ (bad) delay I've ever had.
3   We cancelled the contract. It was _____ (good) decision in the situation.
4   Diane took the train to Paris from London. It was _____ (fast) option.
5   We decided to use the Hotel Orbis for our conference. It was _____ (suitable) hotel.
6   This building is _____ (expensive) our company has built.

First conditional 第一類條件句

肯定形式：

*   If **I see** Mr. Field, **I'll (I will) give** him the message.
*   If he**'s** (he **is**) in the office, he**'ll** (he **will**) **call** you.
*   If they**'re** (they **are**) late, they**'ll** (they **will**) **miss** their flight.

否定形式：

*   If it **isn't** (**is not**) ready, she**'ll** (she **will**) come later.

提問：

*   What**'ll** (what **will**) you do if the train **is cancelled**?
*   **Will** she **be able to see** me if I come to the office?

長答案：

*   **I'll** (I **will**) **take** a taxi.

短答案：

*   Yes, you **will**.
*   No, you **won't** (**will not**).

條件句含兩部份或兩個從句：if- 從句和結果從句。第一條件句用於描述有可能或將來預期的結果。

*   If the train is late, we**'ll take** a taxi.

if- 從句用一般現在式，而結果從句用 will / won't + 不定式。兩個從句的次序可互換，若以結果從句為首，則無需逗號：

- We**'ll telephone** Diane **if** we **have** time.
- **If** we **have** time, we**'ll telephone** Diane.

Exercise 12

配對句子的兩部份。

1	If the weather's good,	A	the drive will take about twenty minutes.
2	We'll come to the meeting	B	if I offer more money?
3	If the roads are clear,	C	we'll work outside.
4	What'll he do	D	if there aren't enough people.
5	We'll have a problem	E	if you arrange a meeting room.

can 用作表達能力

can 和 can't 表示完成某事的能力，可指目前這一刻或一般情況。

- **Can** you **play** golf? (= Do you have the skills?)
- **Can** you all **see** the slide? (= Is it possible for you to see it?)

can 也指獲得准許做某事。

- You **can drive** a car when you're seventeen.
- You **can't eat** food in here.
- He **can sleep** in the living room.

過去形式是 could。

- My daughter **could speak** three languages when she was five.
- I **couldn't (could not) understand** anything they said.

will be able to 用於表達將來的能力

- The new BMW electric car **will be able to drive** at 120 km/h.

Exercise 13

使用以下詞語完成句子，可用超過一次。

able	be	can	can't	couldn't

1 My grandmother _____ speak Mandarin perfectly, but she _____ write it.
2 We'll go on the train so we'll be _____ to work together on our way to the meeting.
3 He _____ fly to Boston yesterday because of bad weather.
4 _____ you telephone me in about ten minutes?
5 You _____ sit in here. It's reserved for women only.
6 The Russian spacecraft is so fast it'll _____ able to reach Mars in only a month.

should / shouldn't / ought to 用作推薦

肯定形式：

- You **should see** a doctor.
- She **ought to telephone** him.
- They **should hire** a consultant.

否定形式：

- We **shouldn't (should not) wait** too long.
- They **shouldn't (should not) have borrowed** any money.

提問：

- Do you think he **should do** that?
- What do you think I **ought to do**?

should / ought to 用於勸告或提意見，兩者意思相同但 should 的用法較常見。
should have / ought to have 用於討論過去發生的事。

- You **should have gone** to the meeting.
- We **ought to have paid** the money on time.
- I **shouldn't (should not) have talked** to him about it.

Exercise 14

配對句子的兩部份。

1	You shouldn't	A	known about the strike.
2	We ought to talk	B	bought the building.
3	They should have	C	smoke. It's bad for you.
4	He ought to	D	say in the meeting?
5	They shouldn't have	E	to the supplier about the problem.
6	What should she	F	find a new job.

Time phrases 時間短語

- She'll give you her address **when** she calls.
- I'll help you **after** I finish this report.
- We'll start the meeting **as soon as** the boss arrives.
- We won't wait **until** Paul gets here.

will 不會用在 if、when、until、as soon as 和 after 之後。這些時間短語會與一般現
在式一起使用，而 will 會用於主要從句。若時間短語置於句首，主要從句之前會加逗
號。

- **As soon as I get** to the office, **I'll send** an email.
- **I'll send** an email **as soon as I get** to the office.

Exercise 15

使用框內詞語完成句子。

finished	is	soon	until	wait

1   When the report _____ ready, I'll read it.
2   Karen will start the meeting as _____ as John arrives.
4   After the project is _____, Lowis Engineering will be integrated into APU.
5   I won't start _____ the report arrives.
6   If Diane is late, we'll _____.

Present perfect simple   一般現在完成式

肯定形式：

- **I've** [I **have**] **worked here** for ten years.
- **She's** [She **has**] **done** secretarial work for ten years.
- The manager **has read** your letter.

否定形式：

- I **haven't** [**have not**] **worked** in an office before.
- She **hasn't** [**has not**] **called** a taxi.

提問：

- **Have** you **worked** in London before?
- **Has** my taxi **been called**?
- Where **have** you **put** the brochures?

長答案：

- Yes, I**'ve worked** in London for five years.
- No, I **haven't** [**have not**] **called** a taxi.

短答案：

- Yes, I **have**.
- No, I **haven't**.
- Yes, it **has**.
- No, it **hasn't**.

一般現在完成式由 have 和過去分詞組成。這個時態用於描述過往已完成，並和現在仍然有關的動作：

- Can you help me? I**'ve lost** the key to my office. (= I don't have it.)
- We **have to cancel** our visit because she's broken her leg. (= Her leg is broken.)

- I've read some information about your company. (= I know about the company.)
- We**'ve moved** offices since your last visit. (= The offices are different.)

記住我們説某事發生時，不會用現在完成式，例如有標示完成時間的用語，
如：yesterday、last week、at 10 o'clock this morning、in 2010、last October。

- I'm sure we**'ve met** before!
- **Have** you ever **visited** APU before?
- My boss **has been** to a conference here.
- The company **has been** in the APU Group for over 25 years.

它用於形容事件發生直到現在。提示詞有 just、yet、already。

- **Have** you **sent** the report yet?
- She**'s** just **finished** the email.
- We**'ve** already **had** some meetings with APU.

現在完成式可用於提供消息。

- APU **has bought** Lowis Engineering. (= The date is not important.)

Exercise 16

將句中詞語排成正確次序。

1   York / you / to / ever / Have / been / New?
2   hasn't / contract / signed / She / the.
3   moved / We've / again / offices.
4   contract / company / Sunstone / has / won / The / the.
5   already / to / sent / finished / I've / the / my / report / and / it / boss.
6   he / yet / answered / email / Has / your?

too 和 not...either

- 'I drive a Mercedes'. 'Oh, me **too**!'
- 'We want to go on the Queen Mary II to New York.' 'We do **too**.'
- 'The email system **isn't** (**is not**) **working**.' 'I know. And the Internet **isn't working** either.'

當表達與他人有同一經歷時，可在肯定形式用 too，在否定形式用 not...either。

Exercise 17

配對不同對話裏的句子。

1   I hate this software!

2   We need to have a meeting about this.

3   John seems very tired.

A   Yes, and he's often bad-tempered too.

B   I don't like it either.

C   No, and not tomorrow either.

4 Will you see Diane today?
5 I can't find the email John sent.
6 I really like his car!

D You're quite right. I think so too.
E I do too. It's so fast.
F I can't find it either!

Adverbs 副詞

slow → slowly
intelligent → intelligently
cheap → cheaply

副詞用於描述某事如何發生：

- The team worked **quickly**.
- We make regular adverbs by adding –ly to an adjective or –ily to an adjective ending in y.
- The photocopier prints **quickly**.
- The man fell **heavily** to the ground.

頻率副詞如 always、often、never 常用於主要動詞之前，但用於動詞 to be 之後：

- James is **always** late.

We can put many adverbs after the verb and its object:

- Kim sings **beautifully**.
- Petra closed the window **quietly**.

不規則式：

以 -ly (lonely、lovely、friendly) 結尾的形容詞無需改變：

- She looks **lovely**.

Some words are both adjectives and adverbs:

- He's a **fast** driver; he drives **fast**.
- Tim has a **hard** job; he has to work **hard**.
- The plane was **late**; it landed **late**.
- My boss was at work early; he arrived early.

good 的副詞是 well：

- Hong is a good worker. She works **well**.

Exercise 18

將以下句子的形容詞改為副詞。

1 I shut down my computer _____ (quick) and left the office.
2 She drove home _____ (slow) in the dark.
3 The report was sent _____ (early) in the morning.

4   My meeting was cancelled _____ (sudden) because of illness.
5   The server works extremely _____ (fast).
6   This new program helps us deal with the problems _____ (intelligent).

Passives 被動式

肯定形式：

* These shoes **are made** in Italy.
* Safety helmets **must be worn** at all times.
* The work **will be finished** on time.
* The meeting **was cancelled**.

否定形式：

* The reports **aren't (are not) sent** to headquarters.

主動式用於談論某人做了某事：

* Diane **called** John Carter.

當主語或行為者並不重要或身份未明，但我們仍想描述事件時，會用被動式。

The signal **is sent** every five minutes.

被動式由動詞 be 的正確時態和過去分詞組成。常用於報告、過程描述和正式告示。提及行為者時，會用 by。

* The employees **are trained by** Karen Armstrong.
* The engine **is cooled with** water.

Exercise 19

將句子內的詞語排成正確次序。

1   conference / cancelled / last / The / was / week.
2   package / courier / by / will / The / be / sent.
3   management / are / reports / read / by / the / Her / top.
4   temperature / five / The / checked / minutes / is / every.
5   I / be / driven / airport / to / must / the.
6   with / house / The / is / solar / heated / power.

Answer key – grammar reference and practice
答案 — 語法重點和練習

Exercise 1

1 work   2 is focusing   3 is helping
4 arrives   5 is staying   6 is not feeling

Exercise 2

1 Diane is visiting the APU offices next
month. 2 Aren't you going to the party on
Saturday?   3 I'm afraid we're visiting my
mother this weekend.   4 She isn't arriving
until Tuesday.   5 They're meeting the
President at three o'clock.   6 Is he flying to
LA soon?

Exercise 3

1 do / come   2 come   3 do / work
4 work   5 does / arrive   6 gets
7 does / go   8 takes

Exercise 4

1 I'm   2 going   3 Is   4 to   5 Isn't

Exercise 5

1 finished   2 didn't speak   3 Did / telephone
4 did / do   5 didn't email   6 had

Exercise 6

1 E   2 A   3 F   4 C   5 B   6 D

Exercise 7

1 on   2 in   3 at   4 in   5 on   6 at

Exercise 8

1 much   2 many   3 a few   4 many
5 a little   6 much

Exercise 9

1 have to   2 must   3 have to   4 mustn't
5 have to   6 don't have to

Exercise 10

1 harder   2 better   3 cheaper
4 worse   5 happier   6 more difficult

Exercise 11

1 the biggest   2 the worst   3 the
best   4 the fastest   5 the most
suitable   6 the most expensive

Exercise 12

1 C   2 E   3 A   4 B   5 D

Exercise 13

1 can / can't   2 able   3 couldn't
4 Can   5 can't   6 be

Exercise 14

1 C   2 E   3 A   4 F   5 B   6 D

Exercise 15

1 is   2 soon   3 finished   4 until   5 wait

Exercise 16

1 Have you ever been to New York?   2 She
hasn't signed the contract.   3 We've moved
offices again.   4 The company has won the
Sunstone contract.   5 I've already finished
the report and sent it to my boss.   6 Has he
answered your email yet?

Exercise 17

1 B   2 D   3 A   4 C   5 F   6 E

Exercise 18

1 quickly   2 slowly   3 early
4 suddenly   5 fast   6 intelligently

Exercise 19

1 The conference was cancelled last week.
2 The package will be sent by courier.
3 Her reports are read by the top
management.   4 The temperature is
checked every five minutes.   5 I must be
driven to the airport.   6 The house is heated
with solar power.